THE
BABYLONIAN
TRILOGY

The Cities-States Interrelated Novels

The Babylonian Trilogy
PS Publishing/Black Coffee Press/Weirdo Magnet (2009-2016)

The Song of Synth
PS Publishing/Talos/Skyhorse (2012-2014)

Absinth
PS Publishing/Dalkey Archive (2012-2016)

White City
Bizarro Pulp Press (2015)

Omega Gray
Bizarro Pulp Press, (2015)

Suan Ming
Villipede Publications (forthcoming)

THE BABYLONIAN TRILOGY

Seb Doubinsky

with an introduction by
Michael Moorcock

The Babylonian Trilogy
by Seb Doubinsky

First published 2009 by PS Publishing.
This first paperback edition published in 2016 by
WEIRDO ⊂∼MAGNET
an imprint of Leaky Boot Press
http://www.leakyboot.com

ISBN: 978-1-909849-37-2

CONTENTS

INTRODUCTION

The French have a sense of and a talent for the absurd which only rarely manifests itself in English—Sterne, Peacock, Firbank, William Burroughs, David Britton, Steve Aylett—and is perhaps at its most inventive when combined with a Jewish sensibility. Sébastien Doubinsky, who has already established himself in France, who has lived in America and England and now in Denmark, been a bouncer and an academic, has an enthusiasm for the ridiculous and a talent for ridicule reminiscent of Cendrars and Vian, yet, like all Frenchmen, longs to be a Beatle or a Pistol, preferably, but not necessarily, a living one. For me, he is, therefore, a personification of the best modern French literature and living proof that French culture is alive and well and living in Tours or Nantes, even if it thinks it would rather be living in Liverpool or San Francisco.

Doubinsky is impressively, superbly bilingual, well educated in America and France. He shames the average Anglo-Saxon (or even Anglo-Jewish) writer with his fluency and his cultural reference. Steeped in Balzac and Flaubert, he loves Dashiell Hammett and Robert Sheckley; familiar since birth with Ravel and Messiaen, he listens to Robert Johnson and The Clash, investing them with a meaning and sublety which might escape the average Englishman who, in turn, venerates Django or *Les Triplettes de Belleville*. He engages, in other words, in that eternal

7

love affair, frequently unadmitted, denied or denigrated, between the Anglophone and the Francophone.

None of this, of course, would be worth remarking if Doubinsky didn't have an original talent, if he wasn't astonishingly entertaining. That, of course, is his main attraction.

"*The world was much better when you looked at it from underneath* ..." An observation which informs the work of every thieving poet since time began. Some would say it's the only way to see the world, that the moment the writer ceases to be the underdog he relinquishes his authority—that he substitutes an authoritative tone, like Eliot, for the authority of experience. By experience I don't mean the author has to steal church silver or suffer in a garret (though I've long held that a writer who hasn't been bankrupted or gone to prison at least once has to make greater efforts to convince us) but has to retain that sense of marginalization at any price, if their work is to resonate on as many possible levels.

The Babylonian Trilogy certainly works on many levels, sniffing its way through an imaginary city that is all cities; lifting its leg where it feels like it, loyal only to itself. A loyalty, perhaps, which not all of us have yet discovered.

Babylon, as Bob Marley knew, is noise first. And then colour, of course, and scent. And sex. And every sort of combination and possibility. The home of Lilith and hiding place of the Other. Heaven and Hell. Order and Chaos. Angels and devils. Fame and obscurity. Chips and fish. And, of course, mystery. As Georg Ratner knows, studying *The Book of Gates*, reading the Tarot, looking for answers. Beasts and women. Gods and men. Crime and justice. Blindness and vision. Sleep and wakefulness. Peace. Noiseless peace. Death. And is that Bill Burroughs or Raymond Chandler whispering in the void? Maybe only Jimmy can hear them above the Babylonian babble, the rise and fall of the music of all the cities of the world? Or is it a child's scream? Pain or pleasure? Maybe only good-natured Sheryl knows?

The assassin goes about his work and dogs swim free. They fly back to the godhead, they embrace death. Everything must die. Everything is immortal. This is how the multiverse is represented: By grim men with soft hearts. Soft women with grim heads. Their actions are their secrets. Cassandra spikes up. Life goes on. The dragon dreams he's a machine, a ticket to ride. Louise is a breeze. We walk through a hanging garden; Eden's a biochemical lake; spiders crawl under your skirt. Sailor Jack's staggering home again. Time for one last cup of coffee in the Luxembourg, the Jardins Américains where Doubinsky and I first shared a few hours, thanks to that witting catalyst, book sniffer, first rate guitarist, mighty baby Martin Stone.

Since I can't remember much of that conversation I was probably talking about me. But his conversation, his cover story must have been interesting enough for me to ask to read something he'd written. And this was it. I was impressed. Then Linda and I met Sofie, his talented wife, with Theo and Selma, their children. Then we became friends. But it's fair to say, as is often the case, that the book came first.

What else can I say. Do what I did.

Enjoy.

Michael Moorcock,
Lost Pines, Texas.
23 November 2008.

THE BIRTH OF TELEVISION ACCORDING TO BUDDHA

To Steve Weeks, wherever he might be.

"When this sea of madness turns you into stone,
picture of your life shoots like a rocket..."

SONIC YOUTH

SEARCH
AND DESTROY

WAR

The explosion blossomed in the distance. A huge fireball rolled over the dark trees in yellow fury. Steve hid his eyes behind his hand. A gust of wind enveloped the men, filled with dry heat and the scent of gasoline. He wondered how many they had killed this time—he meant a true number, not the absurd figures announced every evening in the propaganda bulletins. He wanted to know whether they were winning or losing this goddamned war... He would try to count the bodies when he got there—what was left of them, at least. Another group of planes zoomed over their heads, shaking the ground with their dark laughter. Some of the men applauded. Everybody had lost a good buddy since the beginning. Everybody. Two of his best friends had died. Little Joe had gone to non-commissioned officers' school with him. They had the same grades; they were in the same regiment; the same platoon... After the mortar shell hit his manhole, all that was left of him were his stripes. He found them hanging on the twisted branch of a burnt-down tree, some thirty feet away. He told himself that when he came back, he'd give them to Little Joe's mother, or to his girlfriend—there wasn't enough left of him for both. And then they had gotten Stu... Great sense of humor, always ready for a pun when things were looking bad. He never let gloom seize anyone. A bullet in the throat was the punch line to his last joke. God had no sense of humor. Or a very dark one. Go figure. The captain barked an order. They all got up, wearily picking up their bags and weapons, dragging their feet towards the towering flowers of fire and destruction.

COITUS INTERRUPTUS

Bill reached his orgasm the very moment the phone began to ring. His sperm turned into sparkling electric stars as it sprayed inside the girl. "Shit" he grunted between clenched teeth, "shit, shit, shit, SHIT!" The girl moved over to the side as he made his way out of the sheets. "Sorry..." he mumbled, putting the receiver to his ear. The girl said something in response, but it was covered by Sheryl's crackling voice.

"Yes... yes... where? Okay... yes... in fifteen minutes? But I... I... what? Okay, fifteen minutes... OKAY!... I said okay... Oh, one last thing, Sheryl... I hate your guts..."

"Who was that?" the girl whined, watching him get out of the devastated bed.

"My boss. A real bitch." He had trouble putting his right arm through his left sleeve, so she helped him. "Sorry, baby, but I've got to run. You can fix yourself breakfast, if you feel like it..."

"At three thirty in the morning?"

He shrugged, and picked up the heavy strap-bag full of video equipment.

"I'll see you later," he managed to say before she slammed the door behind him. HIS door. Shit! He shook his head as he waited for the elevator. Maybe she would still be home when he came back... Wishful thinking. How many girlfriends had he lost since he began working with Sheryl? Too many already. Sometimes, he really *did* hate her guts. And then again, sometimes he didn't.

REJECTION SLIP

Lee reread the short letter for the fifth time. It was typed, impersonal—and it hurt like hell. But there wasn't anything he could do about it: his name wouldn't be in print this year. He pinned the letter on the wall, next to the 57 others already hanging there like dead bugs, some of them yellowing with the years. Marian walked into the room, her wet hair hidden in a snail-like towel. He sat down on a chair, and contemplated his "conceptualist" wall, as he liked to call it. "Don't worry, darling," she said from the kitchen she had just stepped into, "you'll make it someday. You're the best." He let his head hang down. It weighed a ton. Nobody could understand him. Nobody at all. He felt empty and blank. He had been so sure about that one... He had had such a positive feeling... Marian walked back into the room in splendid nakedness, holding a glass of juice in her hand. She put the glass down on the little bed-table, and began to rummage in her drawer, looking for some clothes. He glanced at the bed. Maybe some animal sex would help heal the wound. It usually did. Marian caught his peculiar look, and swiftly pulled her panties up. "Sorry, Lee, but today I have my period..." He sighed and looked back at the wall. When things went wrong...

DOG

"You're a dog!" she said, and suddenly Waldo realized that it was true. He fell on his

four legs and began to chase her out of the apartment, barking, drooling and growling. When she was gone, he curled up on the carpet and got ready for a nap. Right before falling asleep, he wearily looked up and saw that the world was much better when you looked at it from underneath.

BODIES

The village was empty. Or rather, there wasn't much left of the village. The Air Force had done a pretty good job. Acrid smoke filled the air. Large holes poked the ground, surrounded by scattered bodies, torn and black like strange trees. Steve began to count them mentally. One, two, three. The captain moved cautiously in front of the column, gun in hand. Four, five, six, seven, eight. He told Steve to check a ruined hut. Nine, ten, eleven. Then another ruined hut. Twelve. And another. Thirteen, fourteen, fifteen. "How many did you find?" the captain asked a soldier who was coming from the other side of the village. "About twenty, Sir." About twenty, Sir. *About?* What in the hell did he mean by "about?" Steve felt a rage napalm his heart. What was the point in counting when he was the only one doing it seriously?

"Very well, then" the captain said, "Let's plant the goddamned flag and let's get out of here. The mission is over, guys. We've won."

Steve felt tears of frustration swell up in his eyes. How did he know they had won? How many enemies had they killed so far; did he know that? "About enough" was the captain's favorite answer. Was it really? Then how come they were still here, fighting, uh? When would they know FOR SURE? When would all this nonsense have its meaning finally revealed? He felt the captain's hand on his shoulder.

"That's it, sergeant. We're going back now. Everything is going to be alright." Sure. He nodded through his tears, flowing like quicksilver on his cheeks. Everything was going to be alright, and this war would have no end. If only there had been a way to count...

CRIME SCENE

The blue and red lights gave an eerie look to the building. Electric voices crackled all around. Bill cut through the thick crowd and showed his pass to the policeman standing guard. Sheryl was already there. Her cellular phone hung under her left armpit like a science-fiction gun. She waved at him as he made his way through the scattered black-and-white cars. "Glad you could make it so fast. The ultimatum is almost over." He began to unpack the heavy video-camera. "Who is it? What does he want?" An inspector Bill hadn't noticed answered for her. "The bastard says he's the famous *Cartoon Killer*, and we have reasons to believe him. We finally managed to corner him in there... This time, he's disguised as the Wild Coyote, from the *Roadrunner* cartoons—you know them, don't you? He's up in some apartment, hopefully empty. That's what we think, but he says he's got an hostage. Go figure... We can't take chances..." He paused and lit a cigarette. The flame flickered under his nose like a small explosion. "Anyway, he won't surrender. He's still up there, disguised and all, with a gun. We know that because the janitor got shot. The only thing he wants, he says, is to be interviewed on TV by this woman here—your boss, I gather. We asked her to cooperate with us, to see if we can get him out of the place, and she said ok. So that's what we're at. Good luck to both of you. You can wear one of our bulletproof jackets if you want, although they're not much against an Uzi..."

Bill thanked him politely, although he wasn't exactly sure for what. They were the bait for the shark, the goat for the wolf. He only hoped the hunters wouldn't miss their target.

"Let's go," Sheryl finally said, opening the door to the back stairs, "we're on a mission for BTV."

Following her, he wondered if she was ever scared of anything. Then, suddenly, he smiled to himself. Yes, there was one thing, one little thing that could scare the woman to hell: an unexpected drop in BTV's ratings. Especially during the news.

COLOR N° 1

YELLOW: color of the sun, of blindness and summer. Color attached to the meaning of fear and fire. Too much yellow in a room can lead to mental confusion, schizophrenia or worse. On the other hand, it is said that if you dress up a baby in yellow clothes three days after he is born, luck will be with him all his life. Yellow is the color of the East and South. It is one of the three primary colors. It is only justice to start with it then.

DOG DREAMS

Waldo is dreaming now, sleeping on his favorite carpet. He is in a street, trotting along and sniffing his way through the city. The smells tell him beautiful stories that make him long and ache inside, wonderfully. The sidewalk is full of clues. No more riddles. No more labyrinths. No more fears of getting lost. Waldo is a good dog now, attached to his master—that is, to himself. Waldo smiles in his sleep and grunts with pleasure. He is holding his leash in his mouth.

DOUBTS

He would never make it. He would never see his name in print. He would never be able to get beautiful young actresses in his bed, just because "they loved the book..." He hated his own name, typed in small shameful letters on the first page of the rejected monster. Lee Jones. What a stupid, stupid name. At twenty-seven, he was already a failure. Marian walked by, getting ready to go to work. He watched her move with growing self-pity. She worked as a secretary in a local bank, making barely enough money for the two of them. He had tried to get a job a couple of times, but it had always ended in disaster. His mind wasn't made for trivia. And yet... Wasn't getting published the most trivial thing in the world? Of course, you could argue that no, it was important, especially if you had a message to deliver. But he had no message. Nothing at all. His stories were like the rain, car fumes and elevator music. In a word: trivial.

It had to end, somehow.

He had to be courageous.

He had to face the facts, and come to the one and only conclusion.

He got up from the chair and wearily walked into the room where Marian was brushing her hair. A decision had to be made. He scratched his head and cleared his voice, trying to avoid her interrogating eyes.

"I... I think I'm going to quit writing..."

He paused, waiting for the effect of this melodramatic announcement. Marian gently pushed him aside as she walked out to the bathroom, and gave him a Speck on the cheek. "Oh, cut the crap, dear. I've heard that one before. Go out, get drunk, and tomorrow you'll feel better."

WEATHER FORECAST

Ernest Hemingway put the gun in his mouth and cocked the trigger. "Looks like we're in for some rain..." he mumbled, smiling to himself.

WILE E. COYOTE

They were standing at the beginning of a long corridor, dimly lit by a shady white glass globe. Large and dirty bay-windows gaping on the left-hand side completed the bleakness of the decor.

"Do you think we'll have enough light?" Sheryl asked.

Bill shrugged.

"I brought an extra lamp, just in case. But it should be okay"

He lifted his free hand, and showed her the object. She smiled.

"Okay, let's go, then."

They resumed their careful walk, and stopped right under the yellowish globe. The door was only a few feet away. It was a normal looking door, with paint in large patches. A cold film of sweat glittered on Bill's cheeks. What wasn't he ready to do for Sheryl... The bulletproof jacket squeezed his ribs reassuringly, in spite of what the officer had said.

"Mister Coyote!"

Sheryl's shout made him almost jump through the ceiling.

"Mister Coyote, it's us—I mean, it's me, Sheryl Boncocur, from BTV ! You're going to be on television!"

She turned to Bill as somebody rummaged behind the door, and winked.

"Start rolling," she said.

The door opened slowly. The shadow of a face made a

careful appearance through the opening, followed by the rest of the body. The man was indeed dressed as the Wile E. Coyote of the cartoon series, and his eyes were as yellow and mean. Bill remembered how much the Coyote used to scare him when he was a little kid. The man hesitated then walked a couple of steps towards them. Bill suddenly felt his stomach press against his teeth. The man was holding a woman's head in his left hand. The grotesque costume was splattered with blood.

"You alone?" he growled suspiciously. Sheryl nodded.

"Mister Coyote, could you spare a few words for our viewers?"

Her voice was firm. Not a single sign of emotion—completely professional, Bill thought, admiringly.

The man nodded proudly.

"You can ask me whatever you want. I'm on TV now. That's all I ever wanted, really. To be on TV, you know. I can remember, when I was a little boy, and I used to watch all those cartoons and..."

Bill hoped there wasn't going to be too much trembling in the image. He didn't want to film the woman's head, but he kept returning to it, again and again. She was blonde. She had blue eyes. Wide open, now. Disbelieving. Blood was still oozing from the wound in the neck, shining softly in the dirty light. He zoomed in for a close-up. If they wanted blood, they were going to have plenty of it.

"I always wanted to be on TV. I wanted to be as famous as those cartoon guys, I wanted to live like them, do the things they did, like this, you know..."

He briefly lifted the head to eye-level.

"I went to the TV studios a couple of times, but they didn't want me. They said they didn't hire cartoon characters anymore. That they were all dead. That they didn't even *exist*, can you believe that? It made me sad. Real sad. So I decided to avenge them. And here I..."

A window suddenly exploded, sending glass fragments all around, like a blinding galaxy. The Wile E. Coyote was thrown backwards against the door, repainting it with his own blood. A gun Bill hadn't noticed fell to the ground with a dull sound. But the head was still in the man's hand. He clung to it frantically as he slowly slouched to the ground, his yellow eyes flickering with life's last gleams. Shouts and sirens burst outside. The wounded man began to vomit blood. Sheryl ran up to him, picking little pieces of glass out of her forehead and hair. Bill followed reluctantly, the wire of the microphone being attached to the camera. He almost slipped in the fast-growing blood puddle.

"One last thing, Mister Coyote, for our viewers…Why did you choose to kill all those women? I mean—only women?"

The Wile E. Coyote lifted a weak eyelid.

"I could never stand to see an animal suffer…"

He smiled, coughed up a couple more times, and passed away. Two policemen from the Special Forces rushed into the corridor, guns in hand. They pushed the journalists aside and handcuffed the body, who was still holding tightly to the golden hair of his victim.

FIRECRACKERS

"Watch out!" somebody screamed, as hell's fireworks began to fall in a deadly shower, suddenly turning the jungle into a tragic Chinese New Year's party. The soldiers began to run in every direction, except the right one. The captain fell on the ground, holding his belly. Steve bent over to help him, but a violent shock on his back threw him to the ground. The wet earth felt sweet under his cheek. Little by little, chaos began to fade, and the world whirled slowly out of sight. Everything was peaceful and turning black. So black he couldn't even see his hands. So black he couldn't remember his own name. So black he had forgotten to count.

COLOR N° 2

RED could be color number two. Red is the color of memories and the days gone by. Red is the color of happiness, on the edge of madness and comfort. Red is an important color in Buddhist China and in orthodox Jewish religion. It is the color of women, for obvious reasons. It's a good color to have on one's side. Never underestimate red.

THE NARRATOR

Don't worry, please—this story will finally make sense, I promise. Well, at least, some sense. Nothing is for certain, nowadays. It wasn't always like that. I will tell you the whole story someday, but not now. This is kind of a mistake. I shouldn't have appeared so soon, although I was here all the time. But you hadn't noticed me, had you? Next time, be a little more careful. You never know who can be reading over your shoulder. You have to remember that. It is very important. No, actually, it is much more than that: it is essential. But let me trouble you no more. Go on with this story. Until we meet again.

WHITE WALLS

Snow. A beautiful landscape made of pure, white snow. Cold sun. Steve tried to focus, but he somehow wasn't able to control his eyes very well. A strangely familiar smell made the landscape flicker and vanish. Something like ether, or rubbing alcohol. He raised a feeble hand, but a shrieking pain nailed it back to his side. He was resting on a surface which felt both hard and soft. His fingers tentatively played on the fabric. A bed. He was in a room. A room with white walls. The pain in his body was almost unbearable. This couldn't possibly be Heaven. Or it wasn't at all like what he had learned about in school.

WRITERS ARE BORING

She didn't like Joe. He was always bad news. Lee was pleased to see him, though. Of course. Joe had brought a bottle of cheap whisky over. They were going to talk about art, revolution, the world and rejection slips all night. She was glad she had this work-meeting tonight. She put on her coat and walked towards the door. Lee laughed. Joe poured some whisky in the glasses. She opened the door and slammed it behind her.

"Writers are so fucking boring," she thought to herself, walking down the stairs. "I hate them."

WALDO NEEDS TO EAT

Waldo was hungry, so he went outside. It was raining a little, but he didn't care. He liked the feeling of the bare sidewalk under his bare feet and hands. Two bitches passed him, wiggling their tails. His stomach was gurgling, but he decided to follow them for a little while. Their smell drove him wild. The raindrops on his nose made him laugh. Life was simply beautiful. The two bitches crossed the street and he went his own way. He found a garbage can in an alley, filled to the rim with leftovers from a nearby butcher's. This made him even happier. A man approached him with curiosity. He growled, showing teeth, and the man retreated. Dog was power.

A WORD FROM OUR SPONSORS

BUY DRUGS.

A GOOD IDEA

Lee was getting somewhat drunk. Things didn't look as tragic as they did earlier on. Joe was laughing. Lee was laughing too. The bottle was almost empty. Joe pointed at the rejection slips pinned on the wall of the dining-room. "That's great, man, really great. I should do the same. Except I don't have enough walls for them all..." Lee emptied his glass. Marian had gone to her meeting. The apartment was empty. The glasses were empty. Life was empty. A wave of self-pity overwhelmed him. A vague idea for a story began to take shape in his mind, in which he would be the misunderstood and suffering character. All his stories had been like that, but this one would be different. More real. More "to the point." He was about to explain this, when Joe interrupted him.

"Let's go to *The Sonic* and get trashed."

Lee thought about it for a second. He really felt like telling Joe about his new project, but then again, getting trashed sounded like an even better idea. Besides, he could always tell Joe about it over a glass. Or two.

SHERYL IS TIRED

The television was already on when she walked into the apartment. The faintly musical buzz made her feel at home. Joyce was in the kitchen, preparing breakfast. The smell of coffee and toast flattered her nostrils as she took off her shoes. The *Wile E. Coyote* report was scheduled for the nine o'clock edition. She looked at her watch. It was eight already. "What a night," she thought to herself, and a tingle of excitement and retrospective fear travelled down her spine.

"You look really tired," Joyce said, trying to get a burning toast out of the toaster with a fork. "What were you on?"

Sheryl shrugged and poured herself some of the black liquid into a mug which said "Who's in charge here?"

"They finally got that *Cartoon Killer*. That was okay, though. No, what really got me was getting stuck in the goddamned traffic on the way back. A fucking hour and a half to get here, can you believe it?"

MOTHER MARY COMES TO STEVE

More dreams in the white room. Angels walked in and out, injecting liquids into his arm. Peace and pain. And vice versa, eternally. Sometimes he woke up, his face raining with sweat. Sometimes he felt like screaming, but he couldn't, his teeth clenched in a feverish lock. Sometimes he imagined he was dying, and that Mother Mary, all dressed in white and gleaming with forgiveness, came to him. These were his favorite dreams.

AND WHAT ABOUT THE NOISE?

Noise, in this story, should not be overlooked, albeit forgotten. Noise is in the core of our emotions, even more so than light and smell. Noise is behind every word we say, thing we do or thought we have. Therefore, in order to understand this story to its full extent, you should consider all the noises that exist around you: traffic, music, radios, television games, children's cries, the barking of a dog, supersonic planes, electric guitars, the piano of Schubert, your neighbour's piano, accidental collisions, breaking plates, washing machines, cartoon explosions, and last but not the least, my favorite—silence.

A BEER OR TWO

"Lirrachur is what makes the world go round," Lee said, trying to focus on Joe, who seemed to be dancing around him constantly. "Lirrachur's my life, man... I can't live with... without lirrachur... it's my life... Can't live without... lirrachur... I'd go insane, man... seriously... Com-ple-te-ly in-sane..."

Joe nodded, his eyes searching around.

"Makes the en-tire world go around..."

Lee picked up his glass with a vague hand. Joe took a crooked cigarette out of a crumpled package. He lit it carefully, then turned around and ordered two more beers.

"Com-ple-te-ly in-sane..." Lee muttered, as if to himself.

A DOG'S LIFE

Thinking about it, Waldo wondered why he hadn't been a dog earlier. After all, nothing else seemed to make sense anymore. THIS was for real, not at all like his life before. He stopped to scratch his ear with his foot. A woman bent down and patted his head. Her smell was exhilarating. He began to follow her down the street, sniffing her well-shaped calves. The woman laughed, pulling on her skirt to make him go away. He felt a strange warmth grow between his hind legs. The heels of her shoes echoed the hectic rhythm of his heart. She was still laughing as he danced around her, displaying his fierce erection. It was not until he had grabbed her leg that she began to scream.

COUNTING

Steve picked up the calendar from the little table and flipped through the pages. Nineteen pages had been crossed out with a big red felt-pen mark. Nineteen days! He sighed and let his thoughts wander. War. Explosions. Bodies. There was no way he could count now. His statistics were fucked. He would never know for sure whether they were going to win or lose the game. Until it reached its end, but by then... What was the point in fighting when the picture was so goddamned blurred? He knew he was a soldier. A simple no-good sergeant. A nothing. Causes didn't need to be understood by people like him. And yet... He had joined because he wanted to be a hero, like his father, who had died gloriously on some beach in Europe. Causes were clear, then. At least, some of them were. But now things had changed. They didn't explain things to people anymore. They had told them: "You are going to fight for the eternal interests of Western Culture. You are going to fight for the right to have Coca-Cola in your fridge and gas in your car." They hadn't really said it like that, actually, but they hadn't fooled anybody. Not him, at least. But what could he do, but count? Counting was the only way. He had invented new equations: duration of mission, distance of target, number of bodies divided by the time of his presence on the field of operation, which was now almost a year. He had figures. He had diagrams. They were in a little notebook in his backpack. Probably all burned by now. The conclusion of a year's statistics had been at hand, and now... Only the absurdity remained. From now on, he would have to play along with that. He ripped the pages of the calendar one by one, until they were all spread at the foot of the bed, like the now useless petals of some strange flower.

TWO COOL CHICKS

Lee put his glass down, and missed the counter. It fell and exploded on the ground with a loud BANG! Joe began to laugh, the bottom of his pants soaked in beer.

"Lirrachur... shit..." Lee mumbled, looking down at the disaster. A hand suddenly grabbed his arm from behind in a firm perfumed grip. Two heavily made-up eyes were staring at him, under a peroxide bank. Another blonde face stood a few feet behind.

"Say," the red mouth whispered, "why don't you guys stop talking about literature, and start talking about *us?*"

Joe grinned, and wet his lips with his tongue. Lee felt a mixture of fear and lust rise inside his pants. Marian would understand. Literature was made out of such encounters. All the time. She would understand, he was sure of it. One of the blondes let out a screeching laughter at one of Joe's corny jokes. Yes, he hoped she would understand... He pressed his thigh against the girl's leg, who pressed it back. Literature was a constant sacrifice. Marian smiled and faded away. She had always understood and, after all, if writing was fucking, loving was forgiving.

COLOR N° 3

BLUE is the color of strangeness and tomorrows. It is the color of eyes and oceans. Seven is its number, and the sky is not a window. Painters use blue to express rage and lust. Blue is androgynous. Blue is the last color we will need for now. But blue is always where you expect it to be. For blue is the color of your shadow. Walk on the sunny side of the street on a cold summer day, and you will see.

VISIONS OF THE SLEEPING BEAUTY

Bill undressed cautiously and entered the bed. The heat from her body surrounded him instantly beneath the sheets. He shivered and pressed his body against hers. She hadn't left, after all. He kissed her bare shoulder, poking his half-erect member against her offered cleft, and she sighed in her sleep. God knew he needed this after what he had seen. Her harsh pubic hairs grazed his throbbing rod and, pushing gently back and forth, he managed to penetrate her all the way. She mumbled something which sounded like "bastard" but she was still asleep. He moved into her faster and faster, clutching on her hipbone with a careful hand. He felt her narrow tunnel become stickier, and the smell of sex floated around their entangled bodies. He couldn't take his mind off the severed head in the *Coyote's* hand. He had to forget about it. He had to, he had to. Sharp needles of pleasure were shooting from the bottom of his back. Yellow hair. Blue eyes. Red blood. Stop it. Blue eyes. Stop it. Red blood. Stop it. STOP IT. STOP IT! Think about something else. The girl, here, she was alive. She was waiting for him. She was life. She was love. She was Sleeping Beauty. Remember Sleeping Beauty? Remember? Yes yes yes yes. He remembered. He remembered. The violent spasms of his orgasm woke up the girl.

"What the hell are you doing?" she exclaimed, pulling away from him in one quick jump.

His now flaccid member dropped on his thigh with shame, drooling in abundance. The Sleeping Beauty switched on the light and turned her hard blue eyes on him. Her head was severed from her body, and when she opened her mouth again, he began to throw up on the soft white sheets.

HOLD YOUR FIRE

THE SPIRIT OF THE RIVER

Waldo's heart was beating in his mouth when he reached the river bank. He turned around to look, but the angry mob was nowhere to be seen. If only that bitch hadn't screamed! He fell to the ground, his tongue sticking out, panting. He could still picture the angry faces, the raised fists, the insults, the heavy steps running towards him... He closed his eyes and shivered. His dick ached now, still stiff and towering between his legs. What a waste, he sighed. If only they had arrived a few minutes, no, not even—a few seconds later, and let his love for her squirt on her offered thigh... The river glowed softly in the twilight. A faint smell of fungus and rot rose from the large and quiet green ribbon. Life as a dog wasn't always fun. He trotted to the water and looked at his reflection. His eyes were dark and sad. He stepped in a little deeper. The cold made him giggle and sneeze.

"Here he is! Let's get him!"

They had found him, but Waldo didn't care now. He calmly entered the darkening flow, and the Spirit of the River welcomed him in her silvery arms. When the mob followed him, splashing around with sticks and blind rage, it was already too late. Waldo the dog had become Waldo the fish.

THE BEGINNING OF THE STORY

In the beginning, Something came out of Nothing, Chaos sprang out of Order, and Order was born to Chaos. The God opened his eyes to the world, and so did the Other, brothers as they were. The God had come out of light, the Other out of darkness. Competition had begun, for to everything the God created, the Other gave a shadow. The God created the Universe, the Other its Movement. The God created the Sun and the Moon, the Other the Earth and the Stars. The tragedy had begun, inserted in the very first seconds like a birthmark or a curse. I can see you are beginning to understand. But this is only the beginning. You must be patient and wait, like I always do.

PERSONAL CHOICE

Steve threw his cigarette to the ground, and looked back at the horizon with his infra-red binoculars. Nothing in sight. The heavy gun stood by his side, its nozzle against the sandbags. He had scratched off all the little marks he had carved so patiently on the butt for the past year. He killed without counting now, and had decided not to care. Absurdity had won. The ghosts of Meaning and Victory had vanished long ago since his hospital days. This war wasn't his anymore. He was just here by accident. Ooops, wrong door. He was just doing his job, like all the others. The captain had died doing his job, and so had Little Joe and Stu. And his father. Couldn't forget his father. They could win, or they could lose—who cared? A lot of the guys had decorations by now. But they never talked about it. They were ashamed. He had been given the Silver Constellation, after what had happened with the 9th Brigade, up there in the jungle. But if anybody had asked him why he had got such a distinction, what could he have answered? "Because I survived...?" Not a bad answer, actually. He picked up the binoculars and looked again. Carcasses of a tank column decorated the long road ahead. He caught the uncovered grinning teeth of a napalmed body. Death's laughter. He lit another cigarette.

The private next to him was reading his girlfriend's letter for the tenth time. Tears were running down his cheeks, and he was shaking his head in disbelief. She had got pregnant and married another guy. One of his best friends from home.

Steve took a deep drag and looked at the night. At least nobody waited for him back home. After all, maybe Hell was only a matter of personal choice...

THE SONG OF ELECTRICITY

Blue yellow red blue red yellow blue red blue yellow red yellow red blue red yellow blue red yellow blue red blue yellow red blue yellow blue red yellow red blue electric electricity.

THE MOMENT BEFORE GUILT

Dawn was rising and the streetlights shimmered like little cold fires against the pinkish blue sky. His head was numb and his dick hurt. That girl was really something! Dirty magazine-like pictures flashed in his mind. The smell of her cheap perfume still surrounded him, as well as the image of her wanting mouth. She had accepted everything from him. And when he said everything... Marian never did. Even a simple blow-job. She considered it vulgar, degrading. He had tried to convince her many times of the poetical aspects of fellatio, but to no avail. She was not a poet. She was not a sex queen. She was Marian. Period. And he loved her. Strange thing. He wondered how Joe was doing with his girl. His back was sore from the night. A cab drove by, but he didn't hail it. He felt like walking in the streets for a while, and enjoying it before guilt hit.

GOOD NEWS

Michael Gonzalez swung in his big leather armchair, and put the diet soda down on his desk. There were no windows in the office—he had always been afraid of heights—but three television monitors displayed the urban scenery which could have been seen if there had been the usual apertures. At thirty-three years old, Michael Gonzalez was the youngest satellite TV mogul in the country, and prided himself in his "young, effective television for young, effective people." Sheryl Boncoeur, at twenty-seven, corresponded to the mark to BTV's *image de marque*: attractive, intelligent and merciless.

"Your *Cartoon Killer* piece was excellent, Sheryl, really excellent... How long have you been with us?"

"Five years now, Sir, plus..."

"You can call me Mike"

Sheryl felt a tingle of adrenaline shoot up her spine, and a short attack of goose-bumps granulated the skin of her forearm.

"Five years, er... Mike... plus a year of internship, after graduation..."

"Basically since we started, uh?"

Michael Gonzalez leaned back on his armchair, joining the fingers of his two hands like in a silent prayer, and brought them to his chin. His smile showed a crest of perfectly white teeth.

"Excellent, then! Great image!" he suddenly burst out, as if stricken by grace. Only his secretary knew that he actually practiced this in his office during lunch-breaks, but she was paid well enough to keep it to herself.

"I can see it from here: the young, beautiful BTV journalist speaking to you from somewhere in Southeast China..."

Sheryl felt her blood spread underneath the skin of her cheeks.

"You mean I... I... I got the war... the war correspondent position?"

Michael Gonzalez nodded, and extended a hand.

"Since Robbie's death out there, God bless his soul, I really wondered who could handle the job as well as he used to. And I've finally found out. Congratulations!"

Sheryl squeezed the offered hand. Her legs were trembling. She couldn't believe it. War, at last. The dream of her lifetime. She felt like screaming, or dancing, or both, but she restrained herself and calmly walked out of the office. She smiled to herself in the elevator's mirror, but she was jumping and singing inside. She couldn't wait to tell Bill: fame was finally at hand.

WHITE NOISE

ORANGE

Orange is the color of cheapness and tears. Skies can be orange, as well as the inside of your palms, although an orange knee is unheard of. Color of spheres and rectangles, of everything without corners or circumference. Orange is the color of mystery and rebirth. It is the color of earth, in which the primitives buried their dead, so that they could come back to life.

SURFING ON THE WAVE OF GUILT

Guilt finally hit, and it hit hard, as it always does. Marian didn't say a thing, but her eyes expressed everything. She was sitting upright in the bed, in front of which he swayed uneasily. He knew she could smell infidelity from there. It hadn't been the first time, but he had a feeling this could be the last one—and his stomach let out a faint wail. She rubbed her face with a nervous hand. The room was a cage, dark, tiny and fatal. The sheets reeked of her insomnia, as she was waiting for him, tossing and turning under the cover, while tears of anger dampened the pillow—he realized with some sickly surprise that he couldn't help to be a writer, even in such tragic moments. "How pathetic," he thought, not really knowing to whom or what this was addressed. Her face was pale, and her lips were thin, as if bloodless. She was beautiful. He desired her through his anguish. Sex had repaired so many things in the past... and had injured so many others. He could almost hear her voice speak inside of him. But this silence was worse than anything. She would not get mad at him this time, she wouldn't slap him or insult him, no, he had a feeling those days were gone now. Completely, absolutely gone. "Self-sacrifice" had been erased from Marian's personal thesaurus.

"So...?" he finally attempted.

His voice was weak, similar to the trapped mouse's final squawk. The ocean of guilt submerged him as soon as she finally opened her mouth and, as he felt the waves inflate and crash on him with controlled fury, he realized that this might very well be the definite end of his once-famous emotional surfing skills.

AFTERTHOUGHTS

Bill was walking down 7th Avenue to catch the subway at Melville Central. He was leaving BTV's tower behind him, glowing gloriously in the smoggy twilight. His mind was but a whirl of confusion. Rationally, he should have been filled with exhilarating joy at the idea of their joint promotion. After all, since this war had started, it had been the dreamed launch pad for every self-respecting journalist. Filming death "live" with the excuse of a good cause—wasn't it what journalism was all about?

Sheryl had been so excited about the news that she had actually jumped in his arms and kissed him in the corridor. He had felt embarrassed. No PDA in the office was rule number two. And rule number one was always to feel excited about a promotion. At the cocktail party, thrown in their honor in Gonzalez' office, he had managed to keep up a good front, with the great help of an entire champagne bottle. But hell, he could feel his legs shaking all the time. And it wasn't because of the war, no, he wasn't the least scared of that: he had been in the Albanian mess, and *that* hadn't been a walk in the park either. No, it was Sheryl who scared him.

Since he had been working with her, a dark hole seemed to have been eating at his guts. She had lead them to fame with her twisted and gutsy reports, he couldn't deny her that—but at what price? She was convinced that journalism was a "holy mission" and that that mission was to inform the rest of the good people of this planet of the existence of Death. Sheryl was Death's most faithful apostle. And it frightened him. Before associating with Sheryl, he had always thought that images were about Life, no matter how violent it could prove to be. But Sheryl had shattered his illusions to pieces: images were Death. Period. They were the moving images of its picture book, they told its story, recorded its sounds. They were its atlas and encyclopaedia. They were its propaganda.

He stopped in a liquor store, and bought himself a mickey of vodka. If images were death, booze was purification. Exorcism. Catharsis.

"Bullshit," he thought to himself as he unscrewed the top of the bottle, "bullshit!"

He took a generous swig and shook his head. He had to convince himself. He had no choice. He had to. It was the only way he could hope to keep *some* sort of life in his own images.

BUBBLES

Life was a miracle before Waldo's eyes. Life was silver and wetness, shadow and motion. Water ran along his body, caressing his sides with a thousand sensuous hands. He was surrounded by a curtain of bubbles, bubbles blowing out of his nose and mouth, transparent, perfectly round and delicate, the bubbles of his breath and past life, escaping to the surface in crowded fury, to finally explode and disappear. Bubbles were the answer to everything, he could see it now. Dog was Power, but Fish was Faith.

SOMEWHERE IN SOUTHEAST CHINA

SAND

The helicopter landed in painful screeches, raising blinding clouds of sand all around. Half-bent silhouettes ran away from the camouflaged dinosaur, some carrying suitcases, others dragging heavy bags. Steve cupped a hand over his eyes. The evening sun was still blinding. James R. Burnett, a Second Lieutenant in the 1st Irish Colonial—and his best friend since a bout of drinking in Golden City some three weeks ago—spat on the dusty ground.

"Journaliss!" he hissed between his clenched teeth. "Goddamned blood-sucking journaliss! Wherever they go, they bring bad luck..."

Steve didn't answer, but instead watched the camp commander—Lieutenant Colonel Gianni Spoletto, of the International Command Forces For Peace (ICFFP, for short)—greet the newcomers and shake their hands stiffly, but cordially. In the darkening skies above the tents, the little red spot of a "Search and Destroy" satellite slowly began its silent ascent, blinking rhythmically. One of the newcomers had striking blonde hair, which flew around her face in the helicopter's artificial storm. Jim turned around and began walking back to his tent. Steve followed, somewhat reluctantly.

"Bloody journaliss!" the Irishman was still cursing. "I'll piss on their graves!"

The desert sands around them lay still, watching the military base in peaceful indifference.

BEER CANS AND A COWBOY HAT

The floor of the room was literally covered with a sea of empty beer cans. You swam in them. Three giant-sized garbage bags stood in a corner, also filled with cans. There was a bed and a long couch, half-hidden under some sort of sheepskin. Handmade bookshelves crumpled under the weight of hundreds of paperbacks. A pile of unwashed laundry sat on the relics of a leather armchair strangely matted with dried paint. A television set stood on the ground, and had miraculously escaped being submerged by a leaning pile of magazines. There was a cowboy hat sitting on top of an old mechanical typewriter.

"This is it. This is my room," Joe said, with a large and proud gesture of the arm.

Lee looked around and immediately felt at home.

LILITH

Ah, but everything that must happen happens in the end (this is my rule), and the time had come. One morning, the Other woke up to see that during his sleep, the God had created Man. Man was small, lean and stupid. His actions were limited, and he had no sense of humor. Man was typically the God´s creature, the Other thought, and he could have it.

But little by little the Other came to realize that there was one small thing Man could do, apart from grunting and eating berries, one small and yet essential thing which caused immense pain and jealousy in the very center of his heart: this ridiculous, pathetic and humorless creature could worship the God.

The Other almost went insane when he had realized this. It ate at his guts night after night, and even the stars he had created could not distract him from his thoughts of envy. The God was so proud of his creature that he neglected everything else, even his competition with the Other.

The situation had become unbearable for the Other. All the creatures of the world who had taken refuge under his shadow when the God had abandoned them could not make up for that single wanton creation. Something had to be done and, after many days of procrastination, an idea suddenly sprang into his untiring mind, glowing and burning like new fires on the side of a mountain.

The following morning, next to Man, soft, dark and troubling, awoke Lilith.

A VISION

Waldo was feeling free and wonderful. Other fish surrounded him in the green water, hiding behind seaweeds and rocks. He would have never thought the river to be that crowded. The surface was but a faint memory now—a confused feeling of sadness and fright, nothing good, just illusions and pain.

Everything was so different now, so... easy. Yes, easy was the word. Opening and closing your mouth, watching the bubbles go up, up, up and explode on the surface... This was living, my friends!

A little further up the stream, he noticed a strange dark shape resting on the muddy bottom. It was hidden by a whirling cloud of fish, which moved to and fro like a silvery curtain. He swam closer to take a good look at the object. As he came nearer, he realized with horror that the thing was looking at him too. It was impossible to tell what color the eyes had been. They were now dull and blank, with the consistency of dried egg white.

A tiny fish entered the open rotten mouth like in a comfortable cave and tugged at what was left of the body's lips. Waldo felt his heart miss a beat. "This" had been a woman. She was wearing a blue dress, which rippled obscenely around her bloated body. Two large concrete blocks had been chained to her ankles. A memory of all the soft female bodies he once knew, of the soft lips he had kissed, of the soft breasts he had suckled, of the soft bellies he had so tenderly caressed began to spin in his mind. They were all concentrated, trapped in this body, glued to it like in an old gooey spider-web. He suddenly gasped for air.

Water was not life, water was death—and death scared Waldo to the limits of his soul. He had thought that Dog had the solution of immediacy, and that Fish offered freedom—but now he knew how wrong he had been. There was no way he could escape lust and decay, there was no way he could escape the *danse macabre* which kept on whirling around him. This body was a vision, and you couldn't stop in the middle of a vision. You had to go further—the furthest possible. Air was calling. Air was pure. He proceeded to the surface, in a cloud of bubbles which dispersed the other fish for a minute, but they all came back and resumed their silvery ghost dance.

HOME, SWEET HOME

The smell of gasoline, motor oil and powder woke Sheryl up and for some reason, it reminded her of home. She wondered what Joyce was up to at this hour—sleeping, no doubt. There were eleven hours apart between here and there... She was working as a consultant in a chemical conglomerate. It was a difficult job, a lot of lies and politics—not unlike hers, as a matter of fact—but it was good money, and Joyce didn't mind the extra hours. She was like Sheryl—professional, dedicated and tough. They had met in college and had kept in touch ever since. When a mutual friend had offered to rent them the apartment, it had seemed natural to them to accept the offer. Just as, a little while later, it had seemed natural for them to fall in love. Thinking about it, she could say she was really happy with Joyce. It had never occurred to her how much until now, in the middle of nowhere, surrounded by death and fire. She could picture Joyce in her bed, sleeping with one arm over her eyes and the other over the cover, and she suddenly almost felt like crying. She would never tell Joyce about this—she would have laughed at her—but she decided to keep that sudden pang of homesickness in her heart forever.

Bill grunted next to her, and his sleepy head emerged from the sleeping bag. The others had begun to wake up too, moving uneasily in their bags like fat, lazy larvae. An officer in full battle gear appeared at the entrance of the tent and clapped his hands. It was time to go to work. The image of the bedroom slowly faded as Sheryl grabbed her fatigues, and a gate of steel shut inside her ribs.

EDUCATIONAL TELEVISION PROGRAMS FOR THE MASSES

08 AM: GAME
09 AM: GAME
10 AM: GAME
11 AM: GAME
12 AM: NEWS
01 PM: SOAP OPERA
02 PM: GAME
03 PM: SOAP OPERA
04 PM: GAME
05 PM: SOAP OPERA
06 PM: GAME
07 PM: NEWS
08 PM: SOAP OPERA
09 PM: GAME
10 PM: MOVIE
12 PM: NEWS
01 AM: TALK SHOW
02 AM: SOAP OPERA (RERUN)
03-07 AM: PAID-FOR PROGRAMS
(Repeat every day until optimal conditions are reached)

PURPLE

Purple is the color of wisdom and greed. It is universally known to express envy, sexual desire and allergy to money. Purple flowers on a grave signify joy and festivity. Some tribes in the Sebastian Islands are said to consider purple the color of the knowledge of the Gods, but so far it has been impossible to confirm this. Purple is also the color of dreams. People who do not find purple in their dreams are considered medically insane. Purple is the color of the back of your eyes. Press your fingers on your closed eyelids, and you will find Purple. But what will you tell it? You have to be careful with Purple. It doesn't like small talk.

DO YOU SEE ANYTHING?

"Do you see anything?" the Colonel yelled.

He was still a rather young man, with a tense face and scared eyes. His youthful fear was contagious, and Steve could feel it himself. Holding his helmet in one hand and the binoculars in the other, he scanned the flat horizon from behind the sand-bags protecting the deep trenches. Thin columns of smoke swayed in the distance. The barbed wire fields shivered after each explosion. Steve thought about the hell in the jungles of the northeastern front, and how it compared to the sands of the southwestern one. He decided it was a tie.

"I can see nothing, Sir!" he shouted back, throwing himself back down as an artillery shell hit the ground some sixty feet away, sending blotches of sand all over his uniform, and down James R. Burnett's neck.

"When are they going to fire, these goddamned satellites? What did we pay all that tax money for?" Steve hissed.

"Modern technology, man," Jim said, taking a swig of his gourd which was filled, Steve knew, with homemade Irish whiskey. "It does wonders when it works, but then again... it seldom bloody works!"

Another explosion shook the ground, and screams filled the air, coming from the next bunker hole. Steve suddenly felt a hand tapping his shoulder, and he turned around to meet the most beautiful blue eyes he had ever seen in his life.

BLANK PAGE

Lee looked at the beer cans on the floor, then out of the window. He could see fire escapes, and that was about it. His own mind felt like it was filled with empty beer cans and rusty fire escapes. Joe was out, doing something in connection with getting back some money somebody owed him. It had been three weeks now since he had moved in and he hadn't been able to type out one single word yet. He looked at the 58 rejection slips piled up under the couch. The picture of Marian still haunted him.

It was like a blank page, unreachable and taunting. It turned all his stories into laughable puzzles. He had tried to call her up a couple of times—big mistake—and had only managed to mumble a few words to the answering machine. He sighed and lit a cigarette. Suddenly, to his surprise, there were no words to describe the violence of a separation. There were no images to match the feeling of desolation and waste which haunted his soul. There were no paragraphs which could contain the crazy birds of souvenirs fluttering inside your head, waking you up in the middle of the night, sick with reminiscence and want.

He got up and turned the TV on.

There were no stories worth telling compared to Marian. And yet, he didn't want to write anything about her. His adolescence as a writer had been left behind a long time ago—

since Jane and rejection slip #28, as a matter of fact. The time of describing at length one's own pain had long been discarded, or so he liked to think. He put on the Stetson hat, sat in the battered armchair, and opened a beer. Some foam squirted over his jeans. Like spunk, he thought to himself—white, sticky, and lonely.

INTERVIEW

"Excuse me, Sergeant... Er, Sergeant?..."
Close-up on a soldier's face. Mid-twenties, tired look, unshaved. War hero type.
"Kerinsky, Ma'am, Steve Kerinsky."
Noise of nearby explosions.
"Well, er, Sergeant Kertinsky, here we are somewhere in Southeast China, in the middle of a bombing and I..."
"Shellfire, Ma'am, it's shellfire... Watch out!"
More explosions. The camera shakes, goes blank for a second, then resumes filming. The soldier is adjusting one of his shoulder straps.
"Phew! That was close... Anyway, Sergeant Kerbinsky..."
"Kerinsky."
"Kerinsky; right. Anyway, here we are for BTV's special live coverage of the war, and do you know Sergeant that right now, three hundred million viewers are actually watching us?"
"No, Ma'am, I'm afraid I didn't know that."
"And how do you feel about it?"
"I don't know, Ma'am. Sincerely, I don't know..."
Noise of machine guns. The soldier ducks for a second, then stands up again, looking lost.
"Wow, Ma'am, they are near... They are bloody near..."
Voices can be heard yelling in the distance.
"Are you scared, Sergeant? You can be honest with us, you know. Anybody would understand..."

"No, Ma'am, I'm not. Not at all. Honest. This is, er... my life. I am paid for this, you know. Taxes..."

"You mean, your motivation is money?"

Explosions. Sand thrown around. The camera shakes, but holds. The soldier lights a cigarette, offers some to the television crew.

"No, no, don't get me wrong, Ma'am. I'm doing this for my country, above all. But this *is* my job, you understand? It's a job. Like yours."

"And what do you think of this war, Sergeant?"

"How do you mean?"

"Well, I mean..."

Sound of bullets, almost like feedback. They all duck, and wait for a few seconds.

"I mean that you probably know that this war isn't very popular back home..."

"No, Ma'am, I didn't know that."

"Well, now you do. And I'd like to have your personal feeling on all this..."

"I don't know, Ma'am. I mean, I don't even really know why we are here. Some say it's to keep the peace, but where is the peace? Where is it? All I know is that I'm here. Doing my job. And I hope we're winning, because that's what wars are fought for, right? Wars are fought to win. And right now, I don't know anymore. Are we winning, Ma'am?"

Focus on the face of the journalist, a young blonde woman wearing fatigues. She looks somewhat surprised.

"I... I don't know... How would I know...? "

The distant rumble of planes over the scene can be heard. The soldier looks up, and throws his cigarette to the ground. The camera focuses on the face of the journalist again. She has regained her professional look.

"Thank you, Sergeant, it was great talking to you and I hope you all enjoyed the show back home. See you tomorrow, same time, same place. This is Sheryl Boncoeur, live from somewhere in Southeast China, brought to you by the BTV network system, and sponsored by the MacFarlane Chemical Company, *Probably The Best Chemical Weapons In The World*. Thank you for your attention, and good night."

LOVE

The man didn't understand Lilith. She was too obscure for him at times, otherwise too blazing. She scared him, so he left her. The Other was disappointed at first, but then a change occurred in him, and the same change happened to The God.

They suddenly liked talking to Lilith, giving her presents, resting next to her after a long walk by the river, learning things from her. She taught them to laugh and to sneeze, to remember and to ignore. They loved her golden voice, they loved her smooth body, they loved her strange and soothing presence. They loved her, and slowly they began to compete again to win her heart, using night and day, fire and ice, wind and water. But deep inside her heart, she had already chosen, and she knew what was bound to happen. But she also knew that there was no other way. There never is. Trust me, I know...

FRIENDSHIP

Fire had passed, and with it the Angels of Destruction. Steve and Jim lay side by side in the trench, smoking a long-desired cigarette.

"She was beautiful, man," Steve growled, "I mean, her eyes, man..."

"The eyes of death, m'boy, the eyes of the banshee..."

"How can you say that? She looked so... so pure!"

"Death is pure. Pure stainless steel."

"I don't care. I liked her."

"She liked you too. You're good for her business."

Steve put his hands behind his head, looking at the sky. Two satellites were shining far away in the blue curtain.

"Is it journalists you really hate, or is it women?"

Jim smiled, and closed his eyes for a second.

"Both, I suppose."

Steve shook the end of his cigarette. It looked like tiny snowflakes in the desert.

"How come?"

The young Lieutenant shook his head and sighed, a sad smile growing on his face.

"My ex-wife left me for a journalist."

Way up there, in the deep ozone azure, the satellites blinked twice, then moved to their next orbit.

GREEN

But I was about to forget Green, the color of flowers and churchyards, possibly one of the most important colors of them all—and certainly my favorite. Green is your reflection in the mirror, and the cheese you have forgotten in your fridge. Green is also the color of fidelity in marriage and unhappy childhoods. There is nothing more beautiful than a blind man with green eyes. If you want to prevent cheating in a card game, wear green. It is the symbol of the final truth and last hope, when everything else is lost. And everything is, isn't it?

WAR AND MARIAN

The soldier in the BTV interview was even more real than reality itself. There was something almost... literary about him. He looked and talked exactly like a character out of one of Lee's novels. He looked like the hero of his next novel.

And war was a perfect setting for adventure and poetry, because war was precisely what was going on inside him now. War was violence and confusion, gains and losses, medals and mutilations. It was absurd and just, unfair and equitable. War was Marian.

He turned off the volume of the TV set and put a record on. Then he opened the fridge to get a beer. He sat down at his desk, where he began to type, with the cowboy hat still on. The keys clicked like machine gun fire, but on the television screen, war was silent.

HELL

It was the time of confusion and chaos. Nothing but smoke and clouds of sand rhythmically lifted by explosions. Shadows ran around, shouting, screaming, some of them dropping their weapons as they fled. Officers tried to contain their men, grabbing them and falling to the ground as the soldiers struggled to get free. Bodies lay here and there, like forgotten garbage bags. Sheryl was crouching behind a wall of sandbags, shaking with every explosion. Bill was a few feet away, in the same position, but he looked surprisingly calm. Not a muscle seemed to twitch in his body, no sweat marks, no head-jerks, absolutely nothing. She envied him for a second.

So this was Hell, finally.

She had always wondered what it looked like, and now she knew.

Bill fiddled with the camera and turned on the transmitter to the satellite. She could see the tiny red light on the camera indicating that they were "on." He turned around, stood up and began walking her way. He had a strange look on his face, but he didn't look scared or anything. He looked lost and happy to be so. He kept on filming as he got closer to her. She hesitated.

"Bill, what are you...?"

He smiled and brought the wireless mike to his mouth.

"Bill, this isn't transmission time! We are not allowed to do this! Do you want us fired?"

She could picture the millions of viewers suddenly interrupted in the middle of their favorite program—whatever it was at this hour—games, series, sports, anything. Her heart beat faster. Bill's grin was devilish. There was a close explosion and she threw herself to the ground. She was almost trampled by panic-stricken soldiers, but Bill was still standing, microphone in hand, filming. He stooped over her, and she could hear the camera's buzz in between the deflagrations and machine gun fire.

"Ladies and gentlemen," Bill started, his voice both sinister and conceited, an atrocious parody of her own professional tone, in fact, "this is Sheryl Boncoeur, live from Hell for BTV Net—"

He stopped in the middle of the sentence, a surprised look on what was left of his face. An explosive bullet had hit him in the back of the neck, blowing off most of the upper part of his skull. Something snapped inside of Sheryl. Her words blurred and mingled under her tongue, seeping out her clenched jaws in melodious absurdity.

She picked up the blood-and-brain stained camera and began to walk around, filming. The little red light was her Shepherd's star, guiding her through the obscure maze of insanity and violence. It was the only light she saw.

When the rescue helicopters finally landed some hours later, she was still filming, surrounded by a pile of dead bodies which had protected her from enemy fire, singing a strange song to herself. It was only inside the chopper's bulletproof carcass that she began to laugh hysterically, and proceeded to tear her cheeks apart with her nails. Ten minutes of struggle were necessary before she was finally pinned down and given a sedative shot.

Meanwhile, back on the front, after a series of minor malfunctions, the "Search and Destroy" satellites began to fire on the deserted no man's land.

HOROSCOPE

AQUARIUS

WORK: The economy will undoubtedly get better.
HEALTH: Unemployment is going down, and soon we will be at full employment.
LOVE: The West is going to help the Third World develop its handcraft.

ANGELS

"Helicopters!" James screamed, "They've got bloody helicopters!"

"No, angels," Steve screamed back. "They have angels!"

And suddenly there was a big shock as the wings of the angels touched the ground, turning everything into gold. Jim disappeared in the blinding light and Steve felt sucked upwards. He landed some fifteen feet away, miraculously intact, and, without really knowing why, he began to run. He ran away from it all, his boots carrying him further and further away, thinking for him, guiding him, protecting him, he ran with his eyes closed, trying to forget everything he had seen from the day he was born, and even before that, he ran and ran, until he felt his mouth suddenly filling with the long-forgotten taste of the raspberry ice cream of his childhood.

D. M. Z.

CELEBRATION

They were all there this evening: Tom Cornitz, his agent, the publishers, the journalists, the beautiful girls, the other pimply writers—nobody was missing. The room was packed, and yet Lee was feeling lonely as ever. Here, on the 62nd floor of the Babylon Hyatt, in the middle of the reception which was given in his honor as "the new voice for the upcoming generation," he couldn't help but think about Marian.

The novel had managed to nullify her in a way, to push her behind the thick curtain of creation. He had even sent her a copy, with his new address written on the first page, along with a short and polite note to indicate that he didn't really hold grudges, but she hadn't answered. He wondered if she had opened it before throwing it in the garbage can.

WAR AND PIECES had been on the best-seller list for three weeks now, and he was feeling strangely tired of all this. Things didn't quite seem to match his pre-fame dreams. The articles were always beside the point, and he felt that the public's reaction was somewhat out of proportion. "The voice of a generation" "Rage and conflict in the kingdom of love" "A prophet of our times" "A literary genius, or just another dope?"—the literary magazines' headlines seemed attached to his back like ribbons he couldn't get rid of.

Where was Marian when he needed her?

And Joe? He was gone too.

He had left two weeks before the New Babylonian Press agreed to publish Lee's novel. Another heartbreak had made him take his decision.

"I'm going to fight the forest fires in the mountains," he had said, putting his coat on, and lifting his heavy backpack. "You can keep the cowboy hat."

Last summer had been excessively hot, and there had been requests for volunteers everywhere in the country.

"I write better when I'm surrounded by flames," Joe had said with a wink, before closing the door.

A stunning brunette approached him, a glass of champagne in her hand. He remembered later she was a famous model, working for intellectual fashion magazines.

"I love your book," she purred. "It's so... so... revolutionary!"

Tom Cornitz saved him by grabbing his arm and dragging him aside.

"Don't forget the TV show tonight at eleven. And don't drink too much. We're really counting on this..."

An old painted mummy from outer space joined in, also known as Miss Brandford. the world-famous author of HOW TO LEAVE YOUR HUSBAND IN TEN LESSONS and other bestsellers.

"It's good to know that there are others who share the same talent and beliefs in literature," she gargled, her dentures shining faintly under the crystal chandelier. "Quality is such an obsolete word nowadays."

He took a sip from his third whisky and felt the alcohol wrap him like a security blanket. He looked out of the window of the reception room of New Babylonian Press through his pale reflection, which made him resemble a ghost. Some truth at last, he thought to himself bitterly. At the feet of the building, the city lay like a dark carpet embroidered with scintillating embers. He thought about Joe and Marian. Somewhere, he knew, real fires were burning.

THE CALL OF AZURE

Waldo saw the sky appear through the thin curtain of water. He swam faster and faster, surrounded by a frenzy of bubbles. The vision of the body still clung to his feet, like heavy chains. He wanted freedom, not death. There was no way he was going to let water trap him. Dog was lust, Fish was Slavery. He had to carry on. The world had to be explored further, taken to its limits. He was too young, too imperfect still to be content with half-existences. He almost remembered something, like a feeling or an impression of his pre-dog life, but it quickly fluttered away.

When his head ripped open the surface, he let out a cry like a newborn child. Then, extending his wings, he flew towards the blinding azure.

BLACK

Black is the mother of all colors. It is the color of wisdom and playfulness, of God and the Saints. Black is found in the center of your sink, or in the middle of your eye. Black is everywhere and nowhere, at the same time. Everything is relative to Black. It is the true color of sins and holiness achieved. Black roses do not exist, though. And the reason is obvious: to whom would you give such a flower?

FLOWERS, INCENSE AND A LITTLE GIRL

Steve didn't know how long the little girl had taken care of him when he finally woke up. He sat up and looked around. He was in a hut of some kind, with whitewashed walls. Through the open door he could see other huts, but no one walking around, except for the little girl. In the distance, large blue mountains blocked the view, imposing and peaceful. Silence reigned.

The little girl brought him a cup of water. He thanked her, and she took a few steps back.

"How did I get here?" he asked, not knowing whether the child would understand him or not, but surprisingly, she did.

She began to walk around in the room, in mock zombie-fashion. He laughed, and a faint memory ripped through the obscure cloud of his memory. Yes, he could remember walking towards the mountain, as if attracted by some strange and powerful magnet, and collapsing at the entrance of the village. But after that...

He put the empty cup down and tried to stand on his feet. The little girl ran to help him and, leaning on her frail yet surprisingly strong shoulders, he stepped out into the open daylight. The village was empty, completely empty. Not a soul could be seen, but for him and his young nurse. It seemed to have been bombed. Big craters mutilated the ground; some huts had been set afire, others were decorated with shrapnel. They finally arrived at what seemed to be the center of the settlement.

A huge oak tree stood there, in full bloom under the sun,

twisted and solid. There was a small stool at its feet, surrounded by what appeared to be four bushes of black roses. The little girl helped him sit down on the stool and smiled for the first time.

Bowls of food were displayed in a half-circle around him, as if someone had anticipated his arrival.

He suddenly realized that what resembled artificial bushes were actually television sets covered with real flowers. Steve couldn't see any plugs or electrical wires coming out of them and yet they were functioning, their quiet blue light reflected upon the dusty ground.

The young child lit two sticks of incense on top of each one and bowed to him. A strange peace, a feeling of infinite love and despair seized him all of sudden, as if a secret tidal wave of knowledge and emotions had raised from the depths of his body and overwhelmed him. He could remember everything now, from the voice of his mother in the garden, the evenings out with the boys after high school, the first kiss he got from a girl (her name was Maria, and she had beautiful black hair), his father's after-shave, the "Search and Destroy" satellites misfiring as usual, the name of the grocer down the block, the helicopters coming down in flames, the smell of the sea and the color of the lipstick of the last prostitute he had met while on leave in Golden City, Jim's laughter and Irish holiness gained through heartbreaks and pure whiskey, everything and nothing, from hope to panic, from zero to one, all of this and much, much more, while hundreds of other people began to flock in, coming from nowhere, bringing food, drinks and other presents, calling him strange names and bowing to him every five minutes as he began to realize, with unexpected calmness and gratitude, that he was never to leave this place, this stool under the tree and the little girl who was selling incense sticks and sticking the dirty banknotes in the string of her dress, for at least another thousand years.

JOYCE

Sheryl woke up to the siren of a police car zooming down the street, leaving a trail of light and violence behind it. She lifted herself on one elbow and looked at Joyce, who was sound asleep next to her. It was good to be back home, and yet something had changed.

Joyce had come to see her every day at the psychiatric hospital in which they had kept her an entire week for observation and tests. Joyce would sit on the little metal chair next to the bed and gently caress her cheeks while the scars were slowly healing. Joyce had felt so close and yet so far—and it was only tonight that she could understand why, when, after having made love for the first time in what had seemed an eternity for both of them, Joyce had asked her, as innocently as possible:

"So, how was it? I mean, *really*?"

Sheryl had almost heard her soul break like glass inside her ribs, but she had managed to smile and somehow elude the question. Joyce had said that she understood, but now that she was sleeping, Sheryl couldn't help but wonder to what extent she really *did* understand anything, and if it mattered, in the end.

Another police car screamed by and she thought of the television crews already on the scene. She also thought about Bill, and his coffin which now lay in his hometown. His mother had looked good during the interview. Poor Bill. He had never understood anything about anything, but who could blame him now? She would burn another candle for him in church for him. Maybe she would bring Joyce along. After all, it was Sunday tomorrow.

There had also been a message from Michael Gonzalez waiting for her on the answering machine. He had offered her the job of host on a new talk show which was going to be aired next season. It was a great promotion, but she didn't know what she was going to answer. Joyce said that it sounded great. Everybody had seen her reports on the war, and the buzz was incredible. Pain might be rewarding in the end. She kissed Joyce softly on the lips and buried her head next to her face on the deep pillow. Another siren howled in the distance. Yes, maybe pain could be rewarding after all.

THE END OF THE STORY AND THE BEGINNING OF EVERYTHING ELSE

Every story must end, for the end is always a new beginning.

And so Lilith had chosen The Other to be her lover. They met by the river at night, loving each other truly and deeply under the dark foliage. The Other told Lilith stories, and in return she told him truths. They thought that their secret was well kept, but The God, who had a keen ear, had discovered the truth by listening to the trees' songs, and he had been filled with rage.

He gave Man another woman, and gifted them with both death and intelligence. He took me out of darkness and gave me the power I had long waited for—you will know what I mean sooner or later. Then one day, he invited Lilith for a walk, and killed her. He tore her body apart and hung her limbs to the trees near the river.

Unaware of this, as The God had silenced the world with the murder of Lilith, The Other came like every evening to meet his lover and found the bloody remains. The God came out of the river, laughing at his despair, but The Other grabbed him by the throat and dragged him on the blood-stained ground. They fought for days and nights, but finally The Other managed to rip the God's throat open with his teeth, and let his blood flow upwards into the sky. I watched this, and I helped the Other stand on his feet. But since that fateful day, the Other rules this world alone, and he is insane.

WHITE

White is the son and daughter of all colors, and the sister and brother of music. White withers between shadow and light, in which she bathes like a maiden or a handsome young man. White is the color of insanity and happiness, of tenderness and murdering passions. There is nothing brighter than the white of an eye, more mysterious than the white of a tooth, more tender than the white of a bone. Silence is white, too. When you close this book, you will understand.

BUDDHA MEETS WALDO

Waldo had lost track on how many days and nights he had been flying. The world looked so beautiful from up there, in its mysterious successions of mosaics and weavings. One morning, he glided over a small village and saw a big tree in its center, underneath which a man was sitting. He was surrounded by a large crowd of people gathered around him in an approximate half-circle. Long lines of newcomers were slowly progressing towards the village, carrying offerings in their little bundles. Waldo knew that this was the end of his journey and he landed on the man's shoulder, who turned his head and smiled.

"Ah, here you are at last, sacred bird. I shall name you Waldo, and you are the spirit of desire and confusion, and therefore a part of my self. Be welcome."

The man then bent his head down, and so did Waldo, imitating his new-found master. They both fell asleep for a thousand years, while more and more people crowded around them to watch their dreams appear on the holy television sets, laughing, cheering and commenting on what they saw, for generations and generations.

THE NARRATOR, AGAIN

You are wondering who I am, perhaps.

Haven't you understood yet? I am the colors in this text, the mysterious chapters and the thread between the words. I am the sound of the turning of the page, and the silence of your reading. I am with you and within you. I am above and under. I am the song of the trees and the satellites' radio waves, the laughter of Lilith and the wind on the sea. I am the witness and the actor, the culprit and the innocent. I am the last face you see when you fall asleep, and the first one you meet in the morning. In the paper theatre of your existence, I am the candle which sets everything on fire, and watches you crumple and turn to ashes. But I am also the one who takes you by the hand and leads you out of impossible situations. I am the ink in the pen and the bullet in the chamber, the sigh of relief and the cry of despair. I have no name, but many nicknames, of all of which my favorite is, of course, the narrator.

FAME

He was feeling sick. He could barely remember the talk show, but he knew it had been a disaster. Tom Kornitz had told him otherwise, but he knew better. The misunderstanding had been tremendous, beyond his belief. He had tried to explain to them for the hundredth time that WAR AND PIECES was NOT a political novel, but a simple, stupid love story with some kind of war in the background, but they didn't listen. They just didn't listen. The host had smiled and shaken his head, as if he had been listening to a good joke. Another "young writer," whose name escaped him at the moment, had smiled too, and so had the young actress who had been invited to discuss about some charity organization of which she was a member. They could not see. They would not see. They didn't want to see.

They needed a hero.

He wasn't a hero.

He had to stop walking for a second and rest against a street sign. The alcohol he had swallowed all day was getting to him. He burped and resumed his walk. What would Joe think of this? The streets were empty at this hour, and all the bars were closed. Where were the thousand empty beer cans and the old cowboy hat?

He laughed at himself and almost fell on the dirty sidewalk. He was trapped now, like a rat in a laboratory, and he was the only one to blame. He had walked into a cage and given them the keys.

The face of Marian flickered through his foggy mind, and he felt like weeping like a child. Where was she now?

He slipped again and fell this time. Pain felt good. Real pain. Tomorrow was another day. Tomorrow he would have the hangover of his life, and feel more human. He would call up that little actress and have some good times with her. Tomorrow he would start a new book. He had some ideas already, thanks to some of Joe's stories. He wondered if Joe was still alive. It had been a few months since he last heard from him. He would be the hero of his next story. That was the least he could do.

A taste of bitterness filled his mouth, and he had to bend between two cars to vomit. When he finally stopped, he stood up and wiped his mouth with an old Kleenex. Looking up, he noticed a huge billboard on the wall of the building facing him, overlooking a sleazy parking lot. It was an advertisement for some chewing gum or toothpaste, he couldn't read very clearly because of the poor light. There were a beautiful man and a gorgeous woman on it, smiling at him with all the whiteness of their teeth. Squinting his eyes, he finally managed to decipher the slogan, written in huge red and yellow letters. It read:

"HAPPINESS IS HAPPINESS."

YELLOW BULL

To Martin and Lynn, with all my affection.

"Nothing changed, altered or varied"

Don DeLillo

THE BOOK OF GATES, NORTH AND WEST

1.

THE SUN WAS gently striking the surface of the water, making it seem motionless. Only the tiredless whisper indicated the strength of its raging spring flow, bending its back like liquid muscle. Large chunks of grey ice floated away in the distance, ephemeral wrecks. Three policemen, in their impeccable blue uniforms, were throwing up in the water, side by side, like grotesque life-size hand puppets, their caps bobbing up and down in stomach-turning harmony. One of them had puked on his shoe, and was dipping a careful foot in the dark green broth. A long thin trail of vomit was going down the current, making its sinuous way like a strange serpent heading for the open sea. Commissioner Georg Ratner thought about the people on the other side of the ocean who would benefit from this wonderful gift of civilization. He smiled, but he wasn't cheerful. Shivering in the early morning cold, he remembered—with some surprise— that he hadn't always hated spring.

2.

SMELL OF FRESH coffee—sun rays on the apartment's kitchen table—this could be a Sunday—the toasts are burning, but who cares?—memories are like Sundays—unclear, lazy, magical—Barbara is washing her hands in the sink—the sound of her laughter!—the calendar is shining on the wall like clean sheets hanging to dry—this is spring, believe it or not—a season long forgotten—this is spring—try to forget about it again

3.

THE PHOTOGRAPHERS WERE already here, doing their job. Lightning everywhere, like silent storms. He passed the security fences, and stroked his hair backwards. It was humid. There were patches of snow here and there, the rest was mud. His shoes sank deep with each step, and he was careful not to trip. Lieutenant Valentino, his partner, was trodding behind. A young guy, full of talent. He could hear his slight panting at each humid step. "A fucking cold morning to die," Ratner thought to himself. Police officers trampled all around, some of them carrying torchlights. You could see the white cloud of their breath preceding their half-bent silhouettes. Ten or fifteen police cars were parked randomly on the outskirts of the restricted area, lights flashing grimly in the rising dawn.

"We've got an arm!" someone suddenly yelled, from the semi-darkness.

Georg Ratner hurried in the direction of the shout. You always had to start with something, and an arm might not have been the worst thing to start this new day with.

4.

A young police-officer was standing by his discovery, pale and shivering. The bleak circle of his light revealed a strange object, half-broken, incongruous in the snow, a mixture of red, pink and blue, alien and yet horribly familiar.

If you took a closer look, as Georg and Jesse Valentino did, you could definitely see that it was, indeed, an arm. A woman's arm.

"Where's the rest? The main part?" the Commissioner barked at the rookie, trying to shake him out of his stupor.

The young officer pointed weakly to another direction in the wall of shadows, and suddenly began to throw up on himself. Georg shook his head and turned around. No need to embarrass the kid any further. He made a sign to Jesse, and walked towards a cluster of silhouettes who were standing a little further away, by the growling river.

5.

THE CORONER, a middle-aged black man, but incredibly long and thin for his age, got up and took off his plastic gloves. He scratched his head, then calmly lit a cigarette. Ratner imitated him with a cigar. With the tip of his shoe, he lifted the blue plastic sheet which covered the body—or what was left. From here, in the peculiar dim light of the freezing dawn, it looked like a large chopped animal. A pig, maybe.

"Unusually cold for April, isn't it?" the coroner said, putting on some thick leather gloves.

Georg nodded, and let the sheet fall back into place.

"What have we here?" he asked, looking at the ambulance crew lifting the remains on a stretcher, in what looked like an oversized garbage bag.

"Female, between 25 and 30, black hair, identity unknown, cut in half from head to pelvis, then dismembered. Probably raped too, but it's too early to tell. Nice butcher's work."

Georg grunted and noted everything in a little pad, which had his initials carved on its cover in golden letters: G. R. A gift from Laura for his 36th birthday, about six months ago. "So you can catch all these horrible criminals," she had said. Wishful thinking.

"Like the others?" he asked.

The thin man scratched his head and looked in the distance. On the other side of the river, the city was slowly waking up.

"Looks like it," he finally said, breathing out a long trail of smoke, "but who knows? With all the publicity this sicko has gotten from the media, basically anybody could have done it. Only the tests will tell. You'll have to wait for the conclusion of my report, I'm afraid."

"That's okay, Frank. Thanks anyway."

The coroner shook his hand and left. Georg watched his elongated body tower back to his car, carefully avoiding the mud puddles. He looked like a big bird. A strange big bird.

Valentino was interrogating the patrol cop who had found the remnants. A few yards away, a flock of journalists were now fighting their way through the security fences like a flock of vultures. It was time to leave, he told himself, and puffed out a thick grey cloud of cigar-smoke as he left the scene. There was a faint smell of decay floating around. The smell of life. The smell of his life. He smiled. The cigar switched sides in his mouth.

6.

HOW MANY BODIES had he seen in his life? He couldn't tell. First, he had joined the Army, right after High School. There was a war going on then, "somewhere in South-east China." A mission of peace, they had said. He had never seen so many dead bodies, piled up, mixed, unified in mutilation and blood. Couldn't tell the uniforms apart. He could remember a friend who used to count the bodies. Systematically. He drew figures, diagrams, established statistics. He was trying to figure out war, to give it a tangibility through its most obvious manifestation: bodies. He got wounded, and after that, he had stopped counting. The shock, maybe. Or it could have been amnesia. He wasn't the same, anyway. He wondered what had happened to him. They had gotten separated after the offensive on Lin Tsang, when Hell broke loose. He had just disappeared. Maybe he was in some concentration camp out there, now. Still counting. Or up on a cloud, with Baby Jesus, doing the same thing with saints and sinners. Numbers... Murderers cared about numbers. They always knew how many people they had killed, and so did soldiers, and so did cops.

After the Army he had joined the Force. Maybe to put some value on human life (there were worse excuses than that). One or ten murders were the same thing—as a human life was infinite, priceless. Not a statistic. Never a statistic. He always felt sad when he looked at bodies. Like today.

He grunted and pushed his hands further inside the pockets of his coat.

But he also had a part to play, and he would play it all the way through. *"Commissioner Ratner? A tough one."* And he sure was, but death still hit him sideways. A body was work. Pain began with the investigation, when you moved deeper into personal stories. You saw the mess, the cruelty, the waste. And you began to feel empty. Completely empty. Jesse Valentino opened the door of the car. It looked like a hearse. His own personal hearse. Counting? Who had said "Counting?"

7.

JESSE WAS AT the wheel, his back upright against the seat, as usual. His startling blue eyes moved around like careful spotlights. The Commissioner turned the radio on and the Industrial Jazz station began to emit its strange melodies inside the cabin. He could feel the Lieutenant grow tense. It amused him. He liked it when people hated the music he loved. It made him feel special. Barbara couldn't stand it. She would sometimes walk into the dining room and simply turn the record player off. He didn't have this problem with Laura. She didn't mind it, or she simply didn't care. Go figure.

"Good stuff, isn't it?" he teased the young man.

Jesse turned his head towards him, smiling tensely.

The Commissioner leaned back in his seat, marking the rhythm with his hand, flat on his thigh. The sun was slowly blinding its way through the corner of his eye. Traffic was getting thicker by the minute. Somewhere, in this city, an assassin was having wild dreams.

8.

SWEET MUSIC—sweet sweet music—perfume and soft hands—she walks—soft breasts—dark hole—wet hole—seasons move—great hair—and now a $10,000 question—maybe a trip to the pyramids—sexy cheeks—white teeth red teeth—jesus christ god of death—elevator music holy music—i want a mother—be my mother—kill my mother—yes yes yes yes—buddha god of death—knife axe scream penis slit cut axe penis knife scream slit—slit OPEN—scream—semen Semen SEMEN—welcome my son—redemption—allah god of death—this my dream—leave it alone—this is my child

9.

"I THINK IT'S time to quote a poem, "Jesse said, and he did.

The poem said something about life being short. Very *à propos*, Georg thought. Poetry... Jesse Valentino wrote poems in his spare time. He had confided this to the Commissioner about a year ago. He had even published a small collection last fall in some underground press. Under a fake name, of course.

One dedicated issue of *DEATH ALWAYS WEARS RED AND BLUE* sat in his bookshelves, somewhere in his apartment. He had actually enjoyed reading them, although he didn't get everything. Too modern for him. He liked the Classics—all of them. Chinese Classics, French Classics, Russian Classics, American Classics, you name it. He used to read a lot of poetry when he was younger. Especially during the War. But not anymore. He couldn't figure out why. He just didn't. He read philosophy and books about magic and ethnology. Other poems, in a way. The words might have been different, but the riddles were the same, questions and revelations, all of that. Valentino was a good poet, and he lived by the obscure standards of his secret passion. To him, everything had a meaning. It went beyond aesthetics. Words said something, like "good" and "evil." He wrote a lot of poems about that. To be honest, he seemed obsessed with that. But they were good poems nonetheless. Even if they didn't change a thing about the goddamned world. Actually, this was maybe what Ratner respected the most in his young partner: the attachment to a useless passion.

It took courage in this world.

10.

THEY WERE ABOUT half an hour away from the central police station where they both worked. They shared an office on the 19th floor, overlooking other buildings and the insect-like crowd. Georg Ratner often thought about crowds. They frightened him. One of his recurring nightmares had him walking alone against a crowd getting thicker and thicker. He kept on trying to head on his way, but little by little his shoulders were hitting more and more shoulders going the opposite direction. Finally he always found himself confronted to a wall of people—dark, uniform, grinning—about to throw him to the ground and trample him. He would wake up, screaming silently and sweating profusely. He sometimes wondered if this couldn't be some sort of *omen*.

"Do you believe in fate?" he suddenly asked Jesse.

The Lieutenant shrugged and looked at him in the rearview mirror.

"How do you mean?"

"I mean, do you believe that our destinies are all written down in some big book, and that everything that must happen to us is planned in advance?"

The young man smiled and a strange, passionate light gleamed in his eyes. Georg wondered if he looked at women that way, and if so, what their reactions could be.

"Yes, I do. Absolutely."

Georg grunted and looked out of the window.

"You don't, Chief?" Jesse asked carefully.

The Commissioner opened the window and threw his cigar out.

"I believe in dreams, but that's all."

"Dreams?"

They stopped at a red light.

"Yes, dreams. They tell you important things, things you don't notice during the day. They remind you of your own shadow, of your forgotten sides. Many civilizations believed in dreams. The Egyptians, the Sumerians, the Mayans... Even the Hebrews, for that matter. They all believed that the Gods could speak to you through dreams, that they could help you, cure you, guide you... We don't pay attention to them anymore, but they're signs. Real signs. They indicate roads... The Ancients had maps of the Dream World, and some primitive tribes still do... Can you picture that? Maps... That could help us a lot, couldn't it?"

Valentino avoided to look at Georg for the rest of the ride. He remained silent, a tense half-smile screwed on his face, until they finally arrived in the station's underground parking lot. He was always like this when he couldn't understand the Commissioner's theories, especially his "strange" ones, and the Commissioner had a lot of those, in his opinion.

Stretching out of the car, Ratner smiled to himself. Barbara used to tell him that he was crazy. Laura said he was a poet. And what could Valentino be thinking, behind his scary blue eyes? He shrugged and walked towards the elevator, following the Lieutenant's still silent silhouette. Never ask a cop what he thinks, especially those who work with you. That was rule number one in the department, and to his knowledge, there were no others. It should have been the same in relationships.

11.

A WOMAN OFFICER brought them a steaming thermos of fresh coffee a few minutes after they had got back into their office. Traditions were strong inside the department. Georg appreciated that. He put his feet up on his desk while Valentino rummaged through files concerning the other six similar cases. Ratner thought this was useless, but coffee still felt good, and he poured some into a strange-looking mug.

It was white, with his name written on it. Barbara had it made especially for him during a trip to Spain, and it was woven with a strange cobweb-pattern of dried glue. About a year or so ago, it had fallen and smashed on the ground, due to the clumsiness of a Dutch official who had been visiting the city on some diplomatic program. Georg had carefully picked up the pieces—there had been twenty-seven of them, he had counted—and he had spent the following evening gluing them back together. It took him several hours, but he finally managed, and here it was again, in his hand, where it belonged. During the reconstruction of the ruined object, he had discovered within himself an unexpected patience. But thinking about it, this wasn't all that surprising: after all, it wasn't just a cup—it was the very symbol of his life.

12.

A YOUNG SARGEANT with a striking moustache walked in with the mail and threw it on the already more than encumbered desk. Georg immediately noticed the pale blue envelope, and so did Jesse. Their eyes met and Georg picked it up. He opened it and read it rapidly. The Lieutenant was looking at him with inquisitive eyes, half-leaning on the back of his office chair.

"Riban-Riban?" he finally asked, as the Commissioner put the wrinkled paper back into its envelope.

"Yes, himself. You can open up a seventh file."

The Commissioner walked towards the window and, pulling the curtain a little, looked outside. In the facing building a woman was cleaning her windows. She was doing a very good job, wiping the glass in meticulous half-circles with a yellowish rag on which she regularly squirted some cleaning liquid out of a blue plastic bottle. He thought about Barbara and the way she used to do it.

Suddenly, it occurred to him that he had never seen Laura doing it—it wasn't a mistress thing to do, he guessed. Wives were the day-to-day world, the earthly magic, which would send you back sometimes to the primordial women in your life—mother, grandmother, aunt, sister... Tribal links, basic rites. Wives recreated the eternal world, through simple gestures such as cleaning, cooking, or simple words such as "No, not now, darling."

Mistresses, on the other hand, were from a whole different world. The mapped zones of their universe only included the kitchen, the dining room and the bedroom, and day to day life was full of white zones—*terræ incognitae*, unknown territories. It was a dream world of sex and mutilated emotions, where time was counted differently. You spent years with your wife, moments with your mistress. Essential cycles. You live and you die. You love and you betray.

The woman finally closed her windows and a silent flash of light blinded Ratner for a second, making the faces of Barbara and Laura suddenly disappear.

13.

THE PHONE RANG and Jesse picked it up.

"It's for you, the D.A.'s office..."

"Shit," Georg grunted, taking the receiver from the Lieutenant's hand.

"Georg, what in the hell is going on?"

The D.A.'s voice was always sweet, even when he was screaming, and Georg realized at this very moment how much he hated sweet voices.

"I've heard there's been a seventh murder this morning! This is getting completely crazy! Do you think I put you in charge of this investigation for you and your little friends to sit on your fat asses while this son of a bitch terrorizes the city? How many more innocent victims do you need, Georg, before you decide to do something about it (Georg knew there was someone in the D.A.'s office. Otherwise, he would have said "bitches" instead of "innocent victims")? I have the Mayor's representatives right here, in my office ("Ha!" Ratner thought triumphantly), and they are not happy, Georg, not at all... And I understand them completely, so I called for a press conference this evening, and YOU are going to be there with me! That's an order. You put me in this mess, you tell these people why. At five, in my office. And no swearing..."

There was a violent CLICK! on the other end of the line. Georg put the receiver down and calmly lit a cigar. Some smoke got into his eyes, making him wink.

A long time ago—no, make that an eternity ago—he used to love press conferences. He enjoyed the frenzy of questions, the camera flashes, the purring of the television cameras, he enjoyed feeling important and famous. Reporters used to call him by his first name, and crime had become a red staircase to glory.

He walked around his desk and stopped to contemplate the wall covered with old pictures of him and famous people.

A red staircase to glory.

Yes, you could say he had had his days of glory... He had never refused an interview, he had participated in numerous broadcasted debates, even made conferences at universities... People recognized him in the street, talked to him, congratulated him... Even the Egyptian grocer at the corner of his street had begun calling him "Sir..." And one afternoon, the nephew of this man, aged fifteen then, had said: "Someday, I will be as famous as Mr. Ratner..." Famous on television... Famous in the streets... Famous in Egyptian groceries...

He picked up a photograph of himself shaking hands with the Mayor and nodded silently. Valentino stopped reading the file he had in his hand and discreetly looked up, his blue eyes shifting restlessly from the paper to the imposing silhouette of his Chief.

A long time ago. A long, long time ago.

And then...

He smashed the picture frame on his desk, with all his strength. Pieces of glass flew everywhere, one barely missing his eye. A little cut appeared on his forehead, right above his left eyebrow. Blood seeped out in a thin red line. He breathed heavily, slowly coming back to his senses. Jesse sat motionless, the paper shaking slightly in his hands. After a few seconds, he finally put the picture back on the wall, where it hung, twisted and ruined, next to the others already in the same condition.

14.

"WHY DO YOU think this loony writes you?" Valentino asked as they were both rummaging through the files again, looking for some clue, some trail they might have overlooked, anything to finally really start the investigation with.

"I don't know. I really don't. If I did, we'd probably have caught him by now..."

"Maybe he likes you..."

"Maybe he does indeed."

"Don't you think we should start looking in that direction?"

"What direction?"

Valentino sighed, discouraged.

"In the direction of the people that like you. Fans, groupies, I don't know..."

"Groupies, for *me*? Oh Jesse, come on! He probably read about me in the papers, saw me on television, I don't know... And fans! Cops don't have *fans*! And I know for sure *I* don't have any..."

"Well, you got me," the Lieutenant said, showing his teeth in a commercial-like smile.

"What were you doing last night between ten PM and three AM?"

They laughed and Ratner poured some more coffee into his cup. He needed all the stimulants he could get. Especially if he had a press conference in the evening. The thermos was empty. He picked up the phone and ordered some more. If he ended up completely wired, all the better: that would make him look active on television.

15.

"RIBAN-RIBAN," AS he called himself in the letters, was a serial killer who had begun his grisly career almost a year ago. For each victim, he had sent a letter to the Commissioner. As usual, like in all these cases, they were filled with obscenities, incoherent messages and the all-around religious bullshit. He had murdered seven women, all of them—so far—young prostitutes. The easiest victims, of course. He had a peculiar way of butchering them which had earned him a nickname in the media: "The Hacker." They had jumped on the story as soon as they had found out about it, thanks to a leak generously orchestrated through the D.A.'s office. The elections were coming soon, and it was no secret that the D.A. was going to run for Mayor. Every new murder met with tremendous echo, and because of this, the D.A. , thinking about the rewarding consequences of a solved case, had designated Commissioner Georg Ratner as the Investigation Supervisor. Ratner had been a really popular figure some years ago, as he had solved numerous mind-boggling cases. The D.A. thought it would be excellent for his own image to have Ratner under the spotlights again for this case. The idea was strategically sound, and the campaign staff had applauded at the suggestion. There was one little problem though, which they had all overlooked: Commissioner Georg Ratner didn't give a damn about the case.

16.

"MAYBE WE SHOULD go out there and find some witnesses," Jesse Valentino finally suggested, pushing the pile of useless files in front of him.

"We won't find anybody."

"How can you be so sure?"

Georg smiled, and picked up a crystal paper weight, which shone bleakly between his fingers.

"Nobody saw anything. The bastard took all his precautions: isolated girl, isolated place, no witnesses... It's been like that with all the other girls... And a serial killer is always a maniac of repetition. If it worked once for him, he thinks it will work like this forever. And who knows? Maybe it will... Think about Jack the Ripper..."

Valentino leaned back in his chair, shaking his head.

"But there must be a way... Damn it, there must be!"

The light of the window was reflected in the little crystal ball, casting a grey halo on the tip of Georg's fingers.

"Dreams."

"Dreams?"

Valentino's eyebrows raised a little. Although he had been teaming up with Ratner for two years, he often had the impression of working with a complete stranger. Ratner's mind was like a dark, twisted maze in which he sometimes felt trapped, and he didn't like this feeling.

"Yes, dreams."

The Commissioner made the paper weight roll once more between his large fingers.

"I'm sure they can show us who did it. In Siberian tribes, the shaman can dream up the face of a murderer, and the people say he is always right. Why couldn't it work here?"

In spite of himself, Jesse let his mouth drop.

"Of course it can't work! A dream! In Siberia, they... You must be joking, Chief... A *dream*?"

Georg got up from his chair and took his coat.

"Time for a break; I'm starving... But tell me, Jesse, if a dream can't work in this case, what in the world can?"

17.

I CAN SEE him now—surrounded by flames—he is nearing—
the trail of blood is thinning—it is following me like a beautiful
dress—i can see him in my dream as i see him everyday—i can
see him and he can't see me—i can see and he is blind—maybe
he needs some glasses—some glasses for the blind man

18.

IN THE CAFETERIA, Valentino quoted another poem. Something about spring and the loss of love. Ratner spilled some of his coffee on his pants. Through the huge bay windows, he could see that April was changing clothes. A spot of sunshine ran across the table. He felt like crushing it like a roach.

19.

A SUN RAY runs on Barbara's back. He follows it with his hand, and she giggles. She is naked in the blue sheets. The traffic rumbles outside, harmless—still. He plays with her thick blonde hair, closes his eyes and buries his nose in her strong perfume. He knows the name of her conditioner, he knows the name of her facial creams, he knows the name of her deodorant... The atlas of her body... She turns around, laughing and parting her legs. He penetrates her, looking at himself going in. Everything is shining. He pushes in and out, glistening, throbbing, wanting. She has closed her eyes, and a thin smile appears on her lips. Her thighs shake slightly, as well as her generous breasts. He is buried inside her fertile tumulus, like in an ancient grave. Love is pale pink, color of resurrection.

Why were his thoughts about Barbara often so erotic? And why couldn't he think about Laura this way? He had tried many times, but had always failed. Laura was sex at the moment of sex. She was the contingency of orgasm. But Barbara... She still haunted him. And yet, he had to admit that Laura's body was more erotic—firmer, thinner, younger... Always available, never arguing, never questioning... Too available, maybe? But how could you even think something like that? She liked him, she showed it that way. And yet, it embarrassed him sometimes. It was easier, in a way, with Barbara. If she said "no," it was "no." Laura never said "no." She never said anything, just smiled and opened her thighs. Welcoming. Always available... Could this be "love?" A strange and painful smile appeared on his face, but Valentino didn't notice it, still chewing on his sandwich with professional dedication.

20.

A PLAINSCLOTHES OFFICER suddenly rushed through the cafeteria's hall and zoomed to Ratner's table.

"Commissioner, there's been some shit going down on Lermontov Avenue...You'd better hurry..."

Erotic thoughts disappeared as Georg grabbed his coat and followed the officer out of the glass doors. It was funny, he told himself, how much sex and death were always linked.

21.

THE SIX BODIES lay at the feet of the large concrete wall, twisted and raggedy like eerie broken puppets. In the bleak light of the underground parking lot, Georg Ratner could distinguish very clearly the dark puddle seeping under the parked cars. For the second time in the day, cameras flashed, cops walked around with torchlights, and the coroner shook his head.

"Too late for these ones. AK 49s, no doubt. Look at these impacts on the wall and on those cars... They didn't stand a chance..."

Georg looked at the children lying on the ground. Twelve, thirteen year olds, maybe a little younger, maybe a little older. All of a different ethnic origin, mixed-blood gangs. A new thing, but the same old, crazy violence. He kneeled down, careful not to stain his pants, and searched them with an expert hand. He found pellets and powder in small cellophane bags, and two unused syringes. He put the small bags and one syringe in a plastic pouch labelled "evidence," and discreetly put the other in the pocket of his coat.

22.

JESSE VALENTINO WAS shaking his head, and Georg put a hand on his shoulder. As a poet, he was overly sensitive, in the Commissioner's opinion, when it came down to the death of children.

"Come on, now, Jesse, it's too late. We can't do anything. They're dead. It's over, it's completely over..."

He could feel the Lieutenant's body tremble under his fingers.

"I can't help it, Chief: They're so bloody young!"

The Commissioner shrugged sadly and put a cigar in his mouth. The ambulance crew were zipping-up the little corpses in adult body bags. The name of their gang was sewn on the back of their jackets: *THE CELESTIAL HOODLUMS*.

They were celestial, all right, now, Ratner thought to himself, but he didn't smile.

"Death doesn't give a damn about age, Jesse."

"But *why*?"

The Commissioner gently dragged him to the car. Valentino's eyes were shining in the ambulance's lights, and his cheeks were wet, red and blue cascades.

"Why?" he repeated, faintly.

"Because we don't give a damn, that's why. What are six children playing with guns in this city: tell me, Jesse? They're newspaper prose, they're three lines on the back of the paper, they're statistics for the municipality, that's what they are. And that's it! They're the true faces of this city, our faces, and we don't want to see them. We prefer serial killers, and all those sick morons, all those sad clowns out there... They're *something*, at least! We revel in the description of their crimes, we admire their savagery, and you want to know why? Because we've created them, that's why. They're our self-inflicted fears, our own Frankenstein monsters... Why do you think Jack the Ripper went on killing for so long? Because he was in all the goddamned papers, that's why! "

Valentino shook his head slightly. Behind them sirens began to howl.

"But these kids, Jesse, they're nothing. We all know what they died for—drugs, money, power, whatever... They are dirty, mean, desperate, human...—And their death is so completely banal, so completely trivial it doesn't do anything for us. It doesn't make us dream... You want to entertain us? You want the papers to talk about you? Well, dying with a body full of bullets is not enough, no, not anymore... You'd better find something else! Death has to be fun nowadays, Jesse, it's the biggest circus game ever... It has to have imagination potential...

We are bored and we are scared. Death has to make an impact on us, on the market, on sales. It has to make us forget. It has to hypnotize us. Death has to be *live* for us to be convinced that we are indeed alive... You have to be able to buy its stories, bring them home, read about them in color magazines, watch them on your television set... Nobody's complaining, either... You want to know why? Because we all love it, don't we? It makes us feel *good*..."

Opening the door of the car, he suddenly remembered he had a cigar planted in his mouth. But he didn't feel like lighting it.

23.

GEORG STOPPED THE car at the corner of the street. He got out and walked into a liquor store. He came out a few minutes later, holding a brown paper bag.

"Drink this, doctor's orders."

Valentino looked blankly at the mickey of whisky, and shook his head.

"I can't, Chief. We're still on duty..."

The Commissioner put the bottle under the young man's nose.

"It's four twenty. You're off at five. But I'm dismissing you now. So, shut up and drink!"

Valentino reluctantly unscrewed the bottle top and took a short swig. His blue eyes were lost, and, for once, Georg didn't know where.

24.

"I JOINED THE force because I believed in Good and Evil. I see a lot of Evil, and no Good at all. Sometimes, I wonder why I do this job. In the morning, I see a prostitute cut in two; in the afternoon, six kids gunned down. She died because of a maniac, they died because of a series of misguidance and mistakes. Their paths both met today, but I see no light in the trail they left behind. I am confused.

Should I quit, or should I carry on? Is there a meaning behind this bloody door, or is there just another door, endlessly? I wish I had remained as trustful as before, when I still believed in Good and Evil.

Poetry cannot save me now...

But I will carry on anyway, I convince myself of this every morning, even if I have my doubts. Because, after all, doubt is faith, and someone's got to have faith..."

Tapping distractingly his fingers against the plastic steering wheel, Georg was looking out of the window, and paid no attention whatsoever to the Lieutenant's procrastination. Valentino felt somewhat relieved, and took another swig.

25.

HE DROPPED THE Lieutenant at the police station and rushed to City Hall, lights flashing. On the way, he suddenly remembered an exhibit on Egyptian Art he had seen there once, with Barbara, a couple of years ago. Why it had crossed his mind, he didn't know. It just did, and he accepted it as a sort of omen, of a mysterious sign like so many others which had crowded the last three years of his life. They came and went, uncalled for but present, as days went by. He hadn't joked when he had told Valentino about dreams. To him, they were real—and he had good reasons to believe that. Maybe it had been the conversation which had triggered the thought process—from dreams to the soft and mysterious sculpted features of Egyptian art, the distance wasn't very vast.

He could remember the strange statues of scribes and generals, squatting proudly, their bodies covered with mysterious signs—eyes, birds, arms, circles and silhouettes—a strange cosmic alphabet embracing the whole of our existence, but revealing nothing. Hieroglyphics were the words of the Gods, he had read in the exhibit's brochure, and as the Gods could see everything, figures had to be represented in their integrity—as in a "flat" vision. What had struck him so much was that if the Gods could see everything, then why hadn't they made their intentions any clearer? They had given man the signs of the world, but they had forgotten to give him the directions—and meaning always ended up mutilated.

Like the bodies of prostitutes.

He had stopped in front of a huge sarcophagus, larger than man size, made of black schist. It glowed darkly in the middle of the room, imposing and somewhat frightening. On the sides, hundreds of signs had been engraved, among which a very beautiful one, bigger than the others, decorating the front part, where the head of the queen—for it had been a queen's tomb—had laid. It represented a sort of an angel with large wings, holding the moon between her hands, surrounded by nine stars. On the explanation booklet, Georg had read that it represented Noût, the Goddess of the Night, and that the rest of the hieroglyphs were excerpts from something called *The Book Of Gates*. What *The Book Of Gates* was, they didn't explain, but he had never forgotten the name. He stood in front of the large stone piece for a long time, lost in his thoughts. He felt that the darkness within the sarcophagus was calling him. The figure of the Night... Barbara joined him a few moments later and gently broke the spell.

A few weeks later, he began to have dreams that "spoke" to him.

He then understood what Egyptian art was all about: dreams. The signs, the books, the sculptures—they were all referring to the *other* world, the dream world, in which everything also happened. The secret parallel. The Egyptians had known that Life was only the consequence of its own dreams. We had forgotten that, and we were paying for it, every bloody cent of it. Yes, maybe he *was* a little insane—who could blame Jesse for thinking that?—but he *did* trust dreams. It was the only way to escape from nightmares, if it was at all possible to escape from nightmares...

He stepped on the gas pedal.

At least *someone* had to try. Someone with little—or nothing—to lose. Someone who had already lived his own nightmare, and could only welcome dreams.

26.

THE D.A. HAD been waiting for him, and let him inside his office as soon as he arrived. He was smoking nervously and indicated a seat to Ratner, who politely declined it.

"Georg," he began, spreading his hands on the desk and leaning slightly over the files that were artistically displayed in front of him. "Georg, you know how much confidence and respect I have for your work...You are, by far, my best element on the force, and I strongly supported your appointment as General Commissioner of the 27th District... But..."

Georg let his mind wander off, knowing what was to follow. D.A.s were all the same, proud when you broke a case, angry when you stalled. This was the second D.A. of his career, and hell, what could he tell him? Surely not the truth. How would the poor man have reacted if he had looked him in the eye and said: "Frankly, Mister, I don't give a damn about your goddamned Riban-Riban, or whatever he wants to call himself. To me, he's just a pathetic media creation, a dwarf with a big knife, a spoiled brat...You want to catch him? Give every hooker in town a gun, and tell the press to shut up, to stop talking about him, to put the lid on his disgusting little massacres... It would be over in a minute... There are much more essential things happening around, much more tragic...Teenage suicides... Rapes... Drunk driving...You name it... And what are we doing about this, tell me? What are YOU doing about this?"

The secretary showed her pretty face in the door-opening. "Mister Jones, the press is here..."

The D.A. crushed the end of his cigarette in a large crystal ashtray and smiled a diplomatic smile.

"I'm glad to see you agree with me, Georg. I knew we'd understand each other..."

27.

THE FLOODLIGHTS BLINDED him as he opened the door. He raised a hand to protect his eyes. Behind him, he could feel the D. A. pushing his back with his hand. Not a single reporter was missing, he guessed; newspapers, radios, televisions, all there, ready to collect the last drops of his official dribble with a little silver spoon and bring it carefully back to the office, where it would be dissected, analyzed and deformed. As it was expected, they asked him direct questions. As it was expected, he answered sideways.

The D. A. stood next to him, smiling. The game lasted a little more than ten minutes, a game of illusions in which both sides knew how the other was cheating. There was no point in watching the news tonight. He already knew what they were going to sound like. The election machine could purr comfortably. The D. A. was going to be elected. The old mayor thrown down on his ear. The assassin would be captured, eventually. Or forgotten. Same thing. Neutralized. The games would go on, and people would keep on dreaming and dying. The river would keep on flowing in the middle of the city, and the Commissioner would be appointed (some day) Commissioner-in-Chief. The Wheel kept on turning. It was beginning to get rusty, but it kept on turning just the same. He smiled between questions.

His collar was wet with sweat, but he wasn't nervous, just hot. The floodlights. His blood felt like burning lead. It was a good feeling to know that he was alive. But this, the journalists wouldn't understand. Alive wasn't inscribed in their dictionaries, an unknown word, erased from their computer files. They turned the words of flesh and doubt into messages of blood and pain. Let it be. He gave them nasty details about the killings. He lied about clues. He said that the D. A.'s office was doing the best they could (the truth, sort of...). He rejected a few harmless questions, for their quota of cheap mystery and easy effect... He played the game, from A to Z, without any effort of imagination, or second thoughts; he played, purely and simply, like a good trained police dog he was, and they all looked so pathetically grateful when he finally said, with his best paternal grin: *Thank you; that'll be all.*

28.

IN THE CAR, finally alone, he cranked the radio. Islamic Jazz was on. The curves and repetitious rhythms lulled his thoughts. Dreams... Murders... Barbara... Laura... Dreams... Murders... Barbara... Laura... The traffic was smooth and easy for once. He began to relax, and hummed to the music. He had the record at home. Home... How could you call "home" a place where only one half of yourself was living? He had never quite gotten used to Barbara's absence, even after three years. He could sleep in their bed now, and didn't have too many nightmares. But for the first year and a half, he had bought a fold-up bed and had put it in the living room.

"Home is where the heart is."

Where was *his* heart?

Could you really call that old wrinkled apple beating inside his chest a "heart?" Laura said you could. Maybe she liked old rotten apples. This woman was a mystery to him. But then again, what wasn't a mystery in his life? He shrugged, and managed to extract a cigar from his coat pocket. Smoke filled the world around him. Shadow-cars glided next to him and shadow-people went about on the sidewalks. A world of shadows, a world of dreams. Here we were again.

Valentino couldn't understand this. Maybe he was too young, or maybe he was too old. His poetry veiled his world, and probably saved him. It could explain everything; turn pain into images, formulate clear questions out of chaos. Yes, poetry was Valentino's salvation. What could be an assassin's, then?

He thought about it for a second, and then gave up. There was no salvation for assassins.

Everybody knew this.

Absolutely everybody.

29.

allah buddha jesus christ he loves me—gives me milk
when i'm dead—gives me flowers when i sing – jesus christ
buddha allah he comes to me with a different woman every
night—pins her on my wall like a butterfly and i cry—and i
cry—and i am saved

30.

THE HOSPITAL WAS a white concrete square, like most hospitals are, built in a residential area of the city. He parked his car among the hundreds of others already waiting there. Pain and suffering were the most common condition in this world. He locked the door, and walked towards a gate with a big "D," like "Death," painted over it.

The nurse welcomed him with a smile. He signed the book for special admittance, and she nodded as he gave her back the pen. He didn't ask for directions and she didn't offer to help him. They all knew him around here. From sight or from reputation. Just as well.

He went to the elevators and waited. Silence was like inside a church. If there had only been stained glass around... All three elevators were taken. A red light blinked suddenly for the middle one. He waited patiently. Time had no importance here. Not for him, anyway. The doors opened with a science-fiction "whoosh!" and an old lady in a wheelchair was pushed out by a solid reddish-blonde nurse. Ratner moved aside to let them pass and the old lady looked at him intensely.

"You are not my son," she remarked before being wheeled away. She hadn't sounded disappointed. It had been a matter-of-fact remark, as if she had told it to herself instead of the world. "*You are not my son.*" He watched her disappear at a corner of the hallway, and stepped inside the steel cubicle.

The eyes of the old lady lingered inside his own, and he rubbed them with the thumb of his right hand to force the image away.

"You are not my mother," he said out loud to himself, to the emptiness surrounding him in the harsh neon light, and he pushed a greasy fat black button.   Now, they were even.

31.

THE ROOM SMELLED of ether and medicine, but he was used to it. The perfusion bags hung quietly, shining mildly in the semi-obscurity. He sat on the metallic chair next to the bed. He carefully took the fragile pale hand in his and began stroking it. The tubes moved slightly, but he knew it was because of his own movements. The body on the bed hadn't made a single gesture for three years, not even a blink of the eye. Nothing. And yet, it wasn't dead. The lines on the little screens of the machines surrounding them showed it. The heart beat. The pressure was normal. The bodily functions worked in a rather satisfactory way. But there was just a flatline for the brain, cutting the black sphere of the screen in two, like a useless equator line.

A worthless planet.

The hand was warm under his fingers, and he brought it to his lips.

Barbara.

The body had a name.

Ratner.

His name.

Barbara Ratner.

Hit by a car one evening, as she was crossing the street. She had gone to the Egyptian grocer, down the block. She had trusted the red light, arms full of brown bags. The driver was drunk and hadn't stopped. Daily tragedy. Three lines in the papers, maybe a little more because he was famous at the time. He had been invited to participate in a special show on television, two weeks later, about "The Dangers of Drunk-Driving."

For the first time in his career, he had declined the offer.

Then another.

And another.

The driver had been condemned to a year in prison, or two years working in a hospital, in the emergency room. He chose the two years. He still worked there today. He loved the job and was still drinking. He said he had found the meaning of his life...

Ratner felt his own hand tremble.

Barbara seemed to be sleeping, but her face had thinned. Her lips were sealed in a mysterious smile, sending painful vibrations all around. This was why he had taken such a liking to Egyptian art after her accident. He could see her smile on the delicate faces of all those statues, sleeping in eternity, protected by their own ruin. And waiting...

The doctors had said there was no hope of her ever recovering consciousness. He had told them to stop the machines, to please stop the machines. But they couldn't. They said they were sorry, and they shook their heads.

He didn't blame them. He didn't blame anybody. Just sat there everyday, caressing her hand for an hour. Speaking to her, whispering memories to her ear, praying to her shut eyes like to his personal wailing wall. If only God hadn't died three years ago...

Some days, he wished she had been killed that day, instead of this. But you can't undo what has been done. Lesson number one: tell it to yourself every morning. He bit his lower lip and caressed her hair.

"If only kisses could bring you back to life, like in old fairy tales... You remember fairy tales, with princesses and dragons? You remember? Yes? I can see you do... "

His words were absurd, he knew it, but he couldn't help it. He had to talk, break the silence of this shrine, fight against the impossibility. Would it only be for honor, or for his sanity—same thing, wasn't it?

He felt the syringe in his pocket.

Nobody had seen him taking it.

A bubble of air in the tubes and she would be in peace forever. And so would he. And so would Laura. His fingers played with the plastic object. He could feel the needle through the cellophane wrapping.

To be free, at last.

All of them.

A wave of cold suddenly seized him, and his body began to shake.

Keep telling stories. Keep a straight mind.

He moved a little more forward, and breathed into her empty ear:"Once upon a time..."

32.

HE LOOKED AT his own face in the mirror of the hospital's bathroom, as he washed his hands, but he didn't see anything there. In the pocket of his coat, the empty syringe lay still. He hadn't had the courage this time. Maybe some other time.

He would first catch the assassin, and then think about the rest.

Keep some priorities in his life.

Life always seemed to need some kind of order. Somebody had told him once that scientists had even found order in chaos.

If chaos itself contained order...

He dried his hands, and then his eyes.

Yes, keep some priorities in life.

Always keep some priorities in life.

THE BOOK OF GATES,
SOUTH AND EAST

1.

THERE WAS NO mail in the mailbox. Not even junk mail. Good. Letters never brought him anything but bad news. It wasn't exactly true, but he liked the legend. His left arm was loaded down with a bag full of groceries. He had stopped over at the Egyptian store on the corner of the street. The old man was sitting behind the counter. The Commissioner was surprised, because it was the nephew who usually worked in the evening.

"Well, Mister Saadi, it's good to see you, but where's Selim? Is he sick?"

The old man let out a heavy sigh and raised a helpless hand towards the ceiling.

"He is sick, but in his heart, may Allah forgive him! He is no good, I want him to go back to my brother's, with the dogs he belongs to!"

Georg laughed politely, but the old man was really upset.

"Last night, he doesn't come home. I worry. I can't sleep. Finally, he comes. You know the hour, Sir? Seven in the morning. He smells of cheap perfume. I want to help him with his coat, but he pushes me! Me, his benefactor! And now, he is still sleeping! And I work!"

Georg tapped the old man's shoulder with a friendly hand.

"The boy's in love, let him be! You too were young once!"

The old man let out a wry smile.

"Yes, but don't tell my wife!"

They laughed, and on the way out the Commissioner almost tipped over a full rack of sunglasses. They were cheap imitations of famous brands, and were sold two for the price of one. He would have to remember that for the summer.

He took the keys with his free hand and opened the door.

Home.

Where was the red carpet?

2.

HE PUT AWAY the groceries in the kitchen and got himself a glass of red wine. Turning on the lights in the living room, he noticed a message on the answering-machine. It had to be Laura. He pushed the button. It was.

She said that she had a PTA meeting, and she was going to be late, and would he be kind enough to pick her up at the school around nine? Otherwise she would take a cab and they could meet at her apartment later. Her voice sounded strange on the machine, as all voices do. He stretched. He had plenty of time before nine. Whistling, he put on a record and sat down in his favorite armchair, a red velvet English armchair, perfect for smoking the pipe—if you did—which wasn't the case for him. He took a look at the room, enjoying the strange mixture of crystalline sounds and metallic rattles coming from the speakers. The bookshelves were overcrowded with books. He read everything: literature, science, philosophy, anthropology, musicology, criminology, you name it. Barbara used to complain about him buying so many books. "One day," she used to say in mock-warning, "all the shelves will crumble over your head, like the walls of Jericho."

The walls of Jericho had crumbled all right, but unfortunately not over *his* head. He raised his glass to the empty armchair standing across the room. "To fate," he said, and took a long sip. Books. Knowledge. He wondered if Valentino read. You could be a poet without reading books, couldn't you? Or could you? They never discussed it. Actually, they never discussed much, apart from work. Jesse was scared of his crazy ideas, he knew that. To be honest, he sort of enjoyed frightening the young Lieutenant. Call it power play. Call it anything you want. To him, it was just provocation. Friendly provocation. Valentino had so many preconceived ideas about life... It was good, in a way. Good and Evil were handy tools to possess. They helped you define your world. They helped you build a safe house. Yes, this was exactly it: a safe house.

A safe house...

He grunted and took another sip. And what about an empty house? The card which symbolized ruin and catastrophe in the Tarot of Marseilles deck was called "*La Maison-Dieu*," the House Of God. You could see a tower struck by lightning. Perfect image. He looked at the deck of cards resting next to him, on a little table. Fate. A gift from Laura, for last Christmas. The phone rang and he got up to answer.

3.

"GEORG?"

He immediately recognized Sheryl's voice. It was clear and soothing as a spring river. Maybe a slightly polluted spring river, to be honest. He liked her, nonetheless. She was a journalist, and an old friend. Or, rather, she had become a close friend over the years. She used to be the spearhead of what was called "Death Journalism." Bold, unafraid and often slightly sadistic reports were her trademark. The public worshipped her. She had climbed the ladder in BTV, the city's best cable channel, at the speed of sound. Even faster. Supersonic. Serial killers, occult financial operations, the war, nothing was too big nor too horrible for her. She touched everything with her weird angle. Nothing scared her, it seemed: one of her cameramen had been killed in Southeast China, during the war, and she had kept on filming. "No morals," was her motto. Everything for the audience—or for the truth, as she defended herself. What was the difference, anyway? Liberal magazines criticized her ways. Moral majority channels ridiculed her. She loved it. She knew she was opening a way, and she had been right: her methods were now taught in schools. Flow, river, flow.

He should have hated her. She represented everything he despised in this world, everything he fought against now. And yet... He knew her well, since he had often been invited to her shows, and he knew the truth behind it all. What had begun as a ruthless ascent to power had been changed by the war. What she had seen there he didn't really know, but she had seen *something*, and that something had caused her secret metamorphosis. She wasn't interested in showing Death anymore, she showed Pain. Her shows were famous for the cruelty of their subjects, the grotesque of their characters, the horror of their stories. She was running a new show, now, a sort of a televised freak-circus, where she invited famous people to discuss gruesome events. She had explained to Ratner that she was trying to show the audience its true face—the monster behind the smile, the murderer behind the husband, the whore behind the wife. And it worked. It was a known fact that there were fewer crimes at the time of her show, and more suicides. Everybody watched it. She was the Prophetess, the Magician, the Black Queen of prime time. War had been the acid on her flesh, her own walls of Jericho. This was the reason why he felt so close to her. They shared the same secret, the secret of pain.

"Georg?"

"Yes," he answered, suddenly interrupted in his daydreaming.

"I saw you tonight on the six o'clock news... Good job!"

He liked her best when she was ironic. He laughed.

"Thanks! No need to tell you who was twisting my arm..."

"Mr. Candidate, no doubt. Frankly, Georg, what is it with all this story? I mean, seven murders and no clues... This seems hardly believable, knowing you like I do..."

"Is this a professional call, or a simple curiosity call? If it's professional, you can call my office tomorrow. You know that."

"Relax; it's only a personal call. I swear."

He sighed and scratched his belly under the shirt. He knew he could trust her. She had proven it to him before, but tonight he didn't feel like talking about it, and he told her so.

"You sound strange, Georgie. You really do. Anything wrong?"

His jaws clenched, and a roller-coaster of pain suddenly gushed through his lips.

"Anything wrong? Anything *wrong*? Well, Sheryl, as a matter of fact everything's wrong! What can I tell you? The world's wrong, my life's wrong, you're wrong! We're all wrong! And especially this lousy killer, who can't even spell my name correctly in his goddamned letters!"

There was a thoughtful silence on the other end of the line.

"I'm sorry, Georg. I really am. I just called to know how you were doing, that's all. I saw you on the news and I thought..."

"It's okay, don't worry. I'm just exhausted. This job is getting on my nerves. The guy's a genius: not a single clue apart from the letters he sends me. Of course, they don't tell me anything. I think we might end up with another Jack the Ripper. Wait until he stops killing. That's what I'm doing, I guess. Wait until he gets tired of it all. Like us. And all these retards who want results... Don't you use any of this, okay? It's personal. If you do, I give the killer your address..."

She laughed. Sun on ice.

"Don't worry, I won't."

"Promise?"

"Promise."

They blew kisses in the receiver and he hung up. They always blew kisses at each other, and he could never remember who had started this ritual. A common thing, perhaps. The spur of the moment turning into habit. Sometimes he regretted that she was a lesbian. Then again, most of the time, he didn't.

4.

HE FIXED HIMSELF a quick dinner, which he ate in front of the television, sound turned off, with a record playing in the background. The Industrial Jazz gave everything a strange tilt, turning the stupid game he was watching into a macabre ceremony. The truth, again.

6.

HE CUT HIMSELF shaving and winced. All this for Laura, he thought. He hated to shave, but she hated his stubble even more. Unfortunately, the odds were in her favor: he needed her. God knew he needed her.

7.

THE NURSERY SCHOOL where Laura taught was located in the north of the city. He had to speed up if he didn't want to be late to pick her up. He lit the cigar stuck in the corner of his mouth and pressed on the speed pedal. The lights of the city began to leave slight trails behind. He thought about the kids she was teaching. All of them were either retarded, or had some crippling psychological problem. It took a lot of courage to work with them: they would never get better. This was perhaps the reason why she had chosen him. She was used to chronic failures.

He had met her almost two years ago, at a funeral.

The deceased had been a young Lieutenant that nobody really liked, not even his own family. He had been murdered by a notorious street gang during an undercover operation. Nothing exceptional; and he had been the worst cop anyway: corrupt, violent and with no sense of humor.

That day, it had been raining mildly, and Laura had an umbrella which they shared. She was the victim's cousin, and she was representing the other half of the family. After the ceremony, they had gone to have coffee somewhere. It was a gloomy day. They both needed comfort. They talked. He never had thought possible to open up like he had done to a complete stranger, albeit an attractive woman, but he had—and she had listened. The rain had been good, for once. She had gently put her hand on top of his as he was telling her about his life, stroking his knuckles with the tip of her fingers. It had seemed completely natural at the time, but when he occasionally thought about it, it sent shivers down his spine. He had told her everything. The words had a life of their own, and his mind slowly followed them, awed and frightened. When he had finished, he realized she had been crying.

"Sorry," she had said, taking a paper-napkin to dry her eyes. "It's been a long day..."

They had kissed and he had fallen, head-first, into a well of darkness and stars. A beautiful and bottomless well, with slippery edges. He was still falling now, but he didn't really hate the feeling, although he had tried to, many times.

8.

HE PARKED THE car on the empty parking lot. He was late, after all, but there was still light in Laura's classroom. He hurried out, cursing. Memories slowed everything down.

9.

SHE RAISED HER head from the book she was reading and smiled. "Five more minutes, and I was going to call a cab," she said, standing up to meet him. They kissed.

"How did it go?" he asked, withdrawing gently from her embrace.

She rearranged her hair and got her coat from the coat hanger on the wall.

"Fine. You know, there's not much to discuss, with these kids... It's more like a social gathering... And what about you?"

He eluded the question with a tired gesture of the hand.

"Same old crap. We'll never catch him. Nobody wants to listen."

There were children's drawings scattered all over her desk. He considered them for a minute, his eyes floating over the quizzical shapes.

"I told them to draw animals," Laura explained, looking for something in her handbag (he could hear the rummaging and the tinting of keys). "It's part of the therapy. Some of them are very good..."

He picked one up and held it to the light.

A misshapen animal was staring back at him. It took Georg a couple of seconds before he recognized what it was. It was a bull, a yellow bull. He liked the drawing. Somehow, he felt close to it. It was like him: strong, mysterious and... weird.

Laura put a hand on his shoulders. He could smell her perfume, a mixture of dried flowers and sweat.

"You like this one? It was drawn by Cynthia. She's five years old and schizophrenic. On the verge of autism. I figured you'd go for something like that."

He put the drawing down and they left the room. Before Laura shut the lights off, he had one last look for the strange animal still glowing under the harsh light.

"Schizophrenia, uh?" he muttered to himself, shaking his head. Laura didn't hear this, or pretended not to. Grabbing his arm, she led him out of darkness.

10.

"YOUR PLACE OR mine?" she asked, making herself comfortable in the passenger's seat.

He smiled, but it looked more like a wince. This joke had been a ritual for two years, and he still hadn't grown accustomed to it. They had never been to his place. He couldn't do it. Barbara's presence pervaded everything. The chairs, the walls, the windows. It was her shrine, even more so than her hospital room. Her chamber in the pyramid. He reigned, sole king, over her silence. No one could be allowed in. No one was. Laura had often said that his attitude was morbid. Maybe she was right. So what? If he had taken her there, would she have understood the pictures of Barbara in every room, pinned on the shelves of the closet, even, so that she would still be smiling at him wherever he went? And what about the dress he would lay every day on the large double bed, and spray with her perfume? Would she have understood that? No, she wouldn't have.

Laura was not a woman of rituals. She didn't believe in magic. And yet, to him

—he couldn't deny her this—she *was* magic, the most powerful kind, the magic of instants and surprises. The magic of spring and things growing. He was caught between the two sides of the same circle, like a lonely star stuck between night and dawn. He started the car.

"So?" she insisted, watching him carefully through the darkness.

"Guess..." he answered abruptly, trying desperately to think about something else to say that would shield him from her painful smile. Looking briefly through the car-window, he noticed that the night had grown foggy, and that you couldn't see the stars. Not even a single one.

11.

SHE WAS HUNGRY, so they stopped at a diner, at the corner of her street. The light was blinding, flattening everything with hyper-realistic precision. Laura ordered some food and a coffee for him while he sat down on a thick red leather couch, which squeaked under his weight. For some reason, his mind wandered off to Riban-Riban. He wondered what the assassin actually *saw*, when he was committing his gruesome crimes. Blood and pain? Holiness and redemption? Guilt and relief? Everything at the same time? Some people had written that the best way to catch a psychopath was to identify with him. Great. Identify with what? Butchery? Laura came back with a plate and two coffees on a tray. The cold chicken leg she was tugging at was of a bluish pink. Pictures from the Riban-Riban files flickered in his mind.

Yeah. Butchery.

12.

WHEN THEY LEFT, it was raining mildly. He thought of the first time they had met, at the cemetery. Drops were drizzling like a quicksilver shower under the streetlights. Valentino could have written a poem about this. A short poem, full of beauty and confusion. He wondered if he could suggest the idea to him. Thinking about his Lieutenant's crazy blue eyes, he finally decided against it. Someone with his eyes could never write about this. Purity didn't fit in this picture. Didn't fit at all.

13.

"I'M EXHAUSTED," Laura said, letting herself fall on her comfortable sofa as he followed her in, "Would you pour me a glass of cognac?"

Barbara preferred gin.

Then again, who cared?

He took off his poured her a drink.

"You look pensive, dear," she said, taking the glass from his hand, and moving a little so he could sit next to her. "Anything wrong?"

Georg grunted and lay back on the couch, extending his legs on the thick Turkish carpet.

"Nothing more than usual," he answered, taking a sip from his glass. He had poured himself a generous whisky, although, usually, he didn't drink much. He looked into the pocket of his shirt and took out a cigar. Laura picked up the remote control and turned on the television.

There was a show about Abu Simbel, a temple that had been jeopardized by the construction of the Aswan Dam. For its protection, it had been lifted up sixty-four meters above its original site, on an artificial promontory. He had read about this in some archaeological magazine, and it had fascinated him. Saving the old gods... Man would never change. Laura wanted to switch, but he insisted on watching it. She put the remote control at the feet of the couch and lay her head on his lap.

A patchwork of color and black-and-white footage, 1963-1964. Workers on the site, walking like over-speeded ants. UNESCO officials, showing diagrams. Maps. More diagrams. The sun, blazing. Egyptian music. More workers, more UNESCO officials, with suits and ties. The two temples (for there were two, he just learned), baking in the desert heat. Face of Amon, smiling. Face of Rê, smiling. A statue of Ramses and his wife Nefertari, holding each other by the arm. Strange eyes. 1965-1967; crucial years. The desert, extending for thousands of miles. The Nile, like a long green worm.

Laura moved, trying to find a better position.

More music. Sunset over the dunes. 1968, the temple is finally saved. The Aswan Dam, at dawn. The Nile, again, crowded with white-sailed ships.

One day he would visit Egypt, he told Laura, who didn't answer.

Workers were cheering, applauding, throwing their hats in the air. One last UNESCO official congratulated himself. More figures, explaining costs and investments. Arabian music, on a final sunset. Credits. End.

Laura was sleeping, snoring lightly.

14.

HE CAREFULLY PICKED up the remote control and switched channels. After a few unsuccessful attempts, he managed to find Sheryl's new show. She was interviewing a writer, a man with little round glasses and a goatee, named Lee Jones. Georg thought he had seen the name somewhere before, but could not place it. He had written a novel, *Red Trails,* which was his third and, apparently, a big success. He looked pale and nervous. The show had already begun and they were discussing a report on something he hadn't seen.

"But tell me, why are you so interested in serial killers?" Sheryl asked.

Before the bearded author could answer, Georg turned the TV off, waking Laura up with the motion of his arm. She lifted herself wearily from his lap and stretched, yawning.

"Let's go to bed," she said.

He nodded, letting the blind eye of the TV set reflect their silhouettes getting up and leaving the room, until they were so tiny they looked like dust specks, disappearing into the greyness of the elliptic screen.

15.

LAURA TURNED ON the light in the bedroom and began to undress immediately, as she always did. He sat on the bed and removed his shoes. Her blonde hair glistened in the yellow light, looking almost orange. A thought about Barbara began to form in his mind, but he sent it back where it came from. It had been a long, tiring day. No need to make things worse.

Laura threw her bra on the chair and began unzipping her pants. Although her back was turned towards him, he could see the fleshy limits of her breasts move along her gestures. She had the motions of a muse, he thought, although he didn't actually know what he meant by that. Every time they had undressed, in this very room, he had thought of the cycle of seasons. Rites of spring. Colors of autumn. She turned around, completely naked, and she smiled. Something in him began to burn, like hay in the summertime.

She came to him and helped him undress.

He loved to feel helpless in her hands.

No more responsibilities.

No more pain.

He closed his eyes, smiling in his turn.

She climbed over him, rubbing her body against his. He kissed her hard mouth, feeling her teeth with his tongue. She licked his neck in return, tickling. Games. Amnesia. She deftly took him in her hand and plunged him deep into her. A slippery well of darkness and stars. Abu Simbel. A yellow bull. 1963-1968. A book. A novel. A glass of whisky. Her hair brushed his cheeks and he saw her face grow tense with pleasure. A glass of cognac. He put his hands on her hips. Rain. She was whimpering now. Silver rain. He felt sweat cover his back. Holy Rain. She bit his shoulder. Holy Rain. Holy Rain. She growled, moving faster and faster. His thighs began to hurt.

Holy Rain Holy Rain Holy Rain HOLY HOLY RAIN!

Silver Holy Rain exploding everywhere in her womb, sending him inside the beautiful dark well of forgiveness and pain, yes, of forgiveness and pain, for-give-ness and pain, again and again and again, cycle of seasons, seasons of pain.

16.

THE TIP OF her cigarette was slowly burning in darkness, and he hoped she would fall asleep without mentioning it again. He mentally prayed for an easy escape tonight, but there was nobody on the other end of the line, and she turned to him after a few minutes of silence.

"Will you give one to me?"

He played innocent, knowing perfectly well it wouldn't work.

"Give one what to you?"

She cuddled up against him and kissed his shoulder.

"You know exactly what I'm talking about..."

He shrugged, trying to shift into a more comfortable position. Yes, he knew what she was talking about, and it filled him with anguish and pain. This was the dark side of the well, the slippery edges. A child. She wanted a child from him. A simple word. A garden. A forest. A labyrinth. A future. A prison.

His nightmare had begun a few months ago, after they had watched a show on television about the widows of police officers. They had not discussed it until they were in bed. He was falling asleep, when Laura had suddenly grabbed his arm.

"And what about me?" she had whispered, in an anxious voice.

"What do you mean?" he had answered, confused.

196

She had sat up in the bed, her arms wrapped around her knees.

"What if you die? What if I became your widow?"

"You wouldn't become my widow," he had said, mechanically, "Barbara would."

There was a frozen silence.

"You know what I mean..." he had tried to apologize.

He could feel a blade of steel plunging into both their hearts. A barbed blade of steel. She had begun to weep, silently. He felt her little jerks through the sheets, and he put a clumsy hand on her shoulder.

"I want a child," she had finally cried out. "I don't want you to ever die on me!"

17.

BARBARA COULD NOT have children.

They had tried to many times, and in the end they had tests taken. The doctors said there was no way. Lightning had struck the house. They had thought about adopting one, but Georg's job didn't make them eligible to be foster parents. Too dangerous. But new techniques were also beginning to work, like artificial insemination. They had talked about it many, many nights. They didn't know what to think about it. The "artificial" side held them back.

They finally had decided to give it a try anyway; "artificial" was still better than nothing. They had just set a date with the hospital when the accident occurred. Ghost smiles of their imaginary offspring scattered all over the street along with useless groceries. Not a single scream. Just the screeching of brakes, and the loud "thump!" of a life shattering into bloody un-matching puzzle pieces.

Drunk driving. No children. Case closed.

18.

HE GOT UP from the bed, stumbling across the room in darkness.

"Where are you going?" Laura asked.

"I need a glass of water," he said, opening the door.

A big glass of cold water, he thought, to wash down all these goddamned children.

The kitchen welcomed him with its peaceful indifference. He poured himself a glass of water, and sat down on a chair. The plastic seat felt cold under his bare skin, and he suddenly wondered if the neighbours could see him from the opposing buildings. Maybe he shouldn't have turned on the lights... He shrugged and drank a sip of the cold liquid. The neighbours could go to hell. It was spring, after all. The season of nakedness, confusion and yellow bulls.

19.

W HEN HE CAME back, Laura was already sleeping. He could hear her calm breathing in the obscurity, and he felt relieved. They would not talk about children anymore. Not tonight, anyway. He carefully slid under the cover, putting a hand under his head. The ceiling was black, cut only by the greyish reflection of the windowpane. He could hear the slow rumble of night traffic outside. Thoughts whirled and shrieked inside his mind, like sparrows at dusk. The warmth of Laura's body was gaining on his right-hand side. She was thirty-six. Barbara was thirty-eight. He was right in the middle, lost at the crossroad, somewhere in a dark forest. He could hear the song of children among the trees. Spirits. Phantoms. He hoped they would stay that way.

He loved Barbara. Laura loved him, but did he love Laura? He had always tried to avoid this question. He had never told her he did, she just took it for granted. A child would have been proof to her. He didn't want a child. Not yet. Not as long as Barbara was still... alive?

He felt his throat drying and he coughed, trying to make as little noise as possible. Laura mumbled something in her sleep, but did not wake up.

Could you say that Barbara was still *alive*?

Was a corpse alive?

She couldn't sing, laugh, kiss. She couldn't walk, speak, hear.

She couldn't complain, cry, or scream. She was just a body in a bed, linked to a world of machines. She was a cadaver with a beating heart. She was just—he hesitated on the word—a vegetable.

An ambulance howled outside, leaving a trail of pain and violence. Familiar sound.

A vegetable...

He turned to the side, breathing heavily.

No, not a vegetable.

A flower.

A unique flower, in a special greenhouse. He had to protect her, take good care of her, because she was invaluable, like some strange South American orchid. Priceless, delicate, beautiful, even in her artificial environment. A flower of memory and life stopped. Frozen in time. Frozen in her Egyptian smile. Forever. Yes, yes, a flower—exactly.

And Laura was...?

He turned around to look at her. She was sleeping on her back, the covers pulled down over her stomach. Her breasts shone mildly in darkness, and so did her lips. He put a careful hand in her hair, stroking it gently. She moaned and smiled in her dreams.

Laura was life in motion.

Healing.

Expectations.

He kissed her soft forehead.

Future eternal.

20.

HE THOUGHT ABOUT the divination deck Laura had given him last Christmas. It had surprised him, for he had never mentioned any specific interest in future-telling. He told her so, but she laughed. They were having dinner at her place, and the candles made her eyes shine.

"Tarot cards are not about the future, dear," she had said. "They're about the world."

He had frowned, puzzled.

"How do you mean?"

She had shaken her hair, and bent a little over her plate.

"All these cards represent something. A multitude of things, like signs pointing in various directions. They indicate ways, knots, side-tracks you might have overlooked... Let me show you..."

She picked up the deck and drew a card at random. He saw her scrutinize it, a look of surprise in her eyes.

"Well, "she said, "that's something..."

She laughed it off and put it back in the deck, drawing a new one. He was going to ask her about the one she had picked up before, but she had begun to speak again.

"Take this one, for instance: The Popess. It signifies earthly things, and knowledge of the occult. Both things are linked and yet are distinct. This is the mystery of the cards. It's also their strength. Do you understand?"

He nodded to be polite. Things were still obscure.

"But how do you *read* them?" he asked, cutting his meat. "I thought there were special ways to read these cards..."

She shrugged and had a strange smile.

"That's true, and yet... There are a lot of different ways. Different traditions... If the cards want to be read, they'll show you the way. But you can always try what the leaflet inside indicates. It's not always bullshit..."

He raised his glass to his lips and took a long sip. He had never suspected such a strange side in Laura. She had always appeared so rational...

"I didn't know you believed in such things," he mumbled, a little confused.

She let out a crystal-clear laugh.

"But I don't! I really don't. I just think it's a good way to look at things around you, sometimes. They make things clearer, they point to other ways, they point to yourself, whatever, but they have no special powers, no magic... They're just cardboard figures and colors, industrially produced, modern, although it is said that cards date back to the Egyptians... Believing in cards! Believing in paper! What do you think I am, crazy or something?"

He felt something strange seize him as they drank to each other's health. A tingle of disappointment, maybe?

Sometimes, he would bring the deck of cards to the hospital and draw them for Barbara. He would look at the rows of images spread on the tile floor, shaking his head and asking Barbara for advice. Her silence was a form of assent, of secret answers, and it often would give him new strengths. Never the same cards. The world was a mess, but it was still a colorful world. Red, yellow, blue... A world of cardboard flames and paper flowers.

21.

A FLOWER AND a deck of Tarot cards.

This was all he had left.

He thought about the syringe in the pocket of his coat.

The Tower, ruin and death.

The Lover, choice and ordeal.

And an assassin.

Never forget the assassin.

The Devil.

The third card.

A crossroad.

A crossroad...

His eyes slowly closed, and he began to snore mildly, his mouth pulled in a tense grin.

22.

HE WAS VISITING Abu Simbel. He had been invited by some UNESCO officials, all wearing blue suits and matching ties. Somewhere, inside the temple, an orchestra was playing. He walked past the six giant statues at the entrance of the temple of Hathor. They were so huge they hid the sun for several seconds as he passed them. The temple was dark, but he could figure out corridors spreading in various directions.

"Follow the arrows," one of the UNESCO officials had told him, "otherwise you might get lost..."

The corridors were half-lit with primitive torches. Someone was walking ahead of him. He looked familiar, although he was wearing Arab garments. Georg caught up with him and Valentino turned around, smiling.

"What are you doing here, Lieutenant?" he asked, surprised.

"I am looking for Byron's lost verses. They were supposedly engraved here... They must be somewhere in here..."

He pointed to a torchlight he was carrying.

"I don't trust these primitive torches. One gust of wind and... That's what happened to poor Byron, you know? Got trapped here and died of starvation. Found his bones, two years later, but not his last poems... I'll find them..." he added, as a mad grin lit up his face. "I'm a poet, after all..."

Georg walked faster to keep up with the young man's fast pace.

"But Jesse, Byron didn't die here! He was killed in Greece, in Missolonghi! He never came here!"

Valentino suddenly stopped and seemed to collect his thoughts.

"Byron? Did I say Byron? I'm sorry, Chief, I meant Riban-Riban."

Laughing, the policeman ran away in a dark corridor, in which he gradually disappeared, like a ghost in a djellabah.

Sweating now because of the heat, Georg resumed his visit, although the corridor seemed to be getting narrower and narrower. There were no more signs in sight. No more painted arrows. He felt like running back all of sudden, but some invisible force was preventing him from turning around.

Frescoes decorated the walls, and the Commissioner, for he was on duty now, wearing his gun underneath his left armpit, took a closer look. They represented a series of seven women, all naked and dancing. A little further up, a man in a white garment was talking to them, giving them money. Sweat rolled into Ratner's eyes, and he had to wipe them before looking at the following scene. The seven women were being chopped to pieces by the man, wielding a primitive form of hand axe.

"Riban-Riban..." he mumbled.

"Yes, Riban-Riban," a woman's voice suddenly confirmed, echoing on the corridor walls like thunder. "Yes, the bastard himself."

He turned around and found himself in a large room made of stone. Straddling a large yellow bull was a woman, completely naked but for a heavy necklace made of semi-precious stones.

"I am going crazy," the Commissioner thought to himself.

"Not yet," the woman said.

She was beautiful but Georg didn't know her.

Islamic Jazz filled his ears.

Her hair was long and black, and her eyes were of a strange pale green, as if made of amber and glass.

"I am Noût," she said, "the Goddess of Night"

"Yes, I know you now," Georg whispered.

"Riban-Riban is here, and you must catch him. You must do this for me."

The heat was becoming unbearable, but he couldn't move from his chair.

"But... why?" he managed to ask, although his tongue was swelling in his mouth.

"I am the Goddess of prostitutes," the woman answered, "and I am the Goddess of memory. I can help you. Watch."

He was in his apartment, sitting on the bed. An ambulance suddenly appeared through the door and Barbara walked out, beautiful as ever.

"Barbara!" he screamed.

She walked towards him, smiling, and took his hands.

They were warm.

Alive.

"Yes," she said, "I am alive."

Laura suddenly appeared from behind and he jumped back, in confused distress.

"Laura? Barbara? What the hell...?"

He suddenly found himself standing in his office. Noût was sitting on the desk and played with the crystal paper weight.

"There is no such thing as choice, Georg. There is no crossroad to wander to, no path to select, no card to draw. Only life prevails, with all its doors. Remember this: there is only life, with its thousand rooms and thousand doors. So why choose? Fate is walking through doors, not choosing corridors, or rooms. You are where you walk, and you are nowhere else..."

Noût smiled, sitting on the huge yellow bull again. The animal was staring at him with his deep black eyes.

A door suddenly opened.

Red foam appeared at the corners of the muzzle of the beast.

A young man was standing in the opening, wearing two pairs of sunglasses on his nose.

There was a fire in the corridor, and smoke filled the room.

Georg let out a loud cry.

"Riban-Riban!"

The youth smiled, and Georg thought he knew this smile.
"Yes, Commissioner?"
Everything went white.
Flames were gushing through the door.
Blinding truth.
Glasses for the blind man.
He could see now.
He woke up screaming.

THE BOOK OF GATES, CLOSED

1.

GEORG LOOKED AT his watch. He was beginning to wonder where Valentino could be, when he saw the young inspector come running at the end of the street. The others were already in place, waiting for the Commissioner's signal.

Valentino was breathless, and sweat covered his forehead, although it was freezing cold.

"One more minute," Ratner said, puffing out a cloud of blue cigar smoke, "and you were going to miss the show…"

The young Lieutenant looked at his watch.

"Sorry, Chief, but I had problems starting my car…"

Georg grunted something and looked around in the street. The Special Forces were all in place, and he could distinguish the silhouettes of the sharpshooters on the roofs, with their infrared scopes. The kid didn't stand a chance… The street had been blocked by police cars and two rookies were directing the ever-growing early morning traffic. Furious horns could be heard, but Ratner didn't give a damn. He looked at his watch again. In less than a minute he would know if Noût had shown him the truth.

2.

Clever policeman clever policeman—come out and play—you have seen the poor boy—but the poor boy has seen you too—dreams always have two doors—mister policeman—and so has fame

3.

A PATROL HELICOPTER was humming high overhead, its blinding floodlight circling around the block. Two Special Forces policemen were standing by the closed door, firmly gripping their semi-automatic weapons.

"How did you find out it was him?" Jesse Valentino asked the Commissioner, taking out his gun in his turn.

Ratner started walking towards the door where a lopsided "Closed" sign hung.

"He should have opened a minute ago, the bastard," the Commissioner grunted. "Something's wrong..."

Valentino followed him closely.

"How do you know something's wrong?"

Ratner spit out his cigar, pulling out his own revolver.

"His uncle would never let him oversleep."

4.

STREETS OF THE city—labyrinth for the blind man—so close and yet so far—trapped like me—exactly like me—two ends of the same rope—but i am saved—allah jesus buddha he loves me—and he hates the blind man—walking in the labyrinth—bouncing off the walls—until he bleeds—and i am saved

5.

"EVERYBODY GET READY!" Ratner said to his walkie-talkie, "I'm going in now."

Standing in front of the dark glass door, Valentino realized they were right in the middle of the chopper's light, buzzing like a gigantic bumble-bee over their heads. Standing in the light as they were, they made a perfect target. He shivered.

"Stupid assholes," he mumbled to the Commissioner, "they're going to get us killed!"

Ratner nodded and shrugged.

"It's too late now, anyway. Let's hope he doesn't have a gun..."

"Let's hope the sun won't be rising today," Valentino whispered bitterly.

Georg nodded to the Special Forces officers standing on each side of the door. In a common gesture they brought their heavy weapons down on the windowpane, which shattered in a loud explosion, sending the "Closed" sign back into darkness.

6.

SHERYL BONCOEUR WAS woken up by the electric chime of her phone. Joyce, her girlfriend of many years, groaned and turned around. Sheryl looked at the red numbers of the digital clock.

"A quarter to seven. Jesus! Who can that be?"

Joyce didn't answer, lost in her dreams.

Swearing, Sheryl finally got up, and almost tripped over her clothes scattered on the floor.

"One day, I will clean up this mess," she mumbled to herself. "One day, I really will..."

7.

THE GROCERY STORE was plunged in thick darkness. One of the Special Forces officers lit a torch light while another looked for a switch. Ratner was walking ahead, one hand extended in front of him, the other holding the gun, drawn back to his shoulder. He could hear Valentino's heavy breathing behind him. He suddenly bumped into something which crashed with a hellish noise. Everybody jumped with fright and surprise, and they waited a few seconds for a reaction—running steps, the click of a gun being cocked, a burst of submachine gun—but nothing happened.

The Special Forces man finally found the light switch to the store, and in a second they were all standing in a blinding white light.

Ratner realized he had knocked over the sunglasses display rack. A sign lay at his feet. It read: "Two pairs for the price of one." Turning to Valentino, he pointed at the sign with the tip of his gun.

"That's how I found out," he said. "Two pairs of sunglasses for the price of one... Ray-ban imitations... Someone who can't spell... "Ray-Ban" times two; there you have it: *Riban-Riban*..."

8.

SMALL CAPS Sunglasses for the blind man—now he can see, alleluiah—all these women, they loved me

9.

THEY CAREFULLY CLIMBED the stairs leading to the apartment upstairs. Not a sound could be heard, except for the steps squeaking under the weight of the men. Ratner was worried because of this lack of reaction. Sweat began to pearl over his eyebrows. At least the old owner should have heard something, with all the stupid noise he had made...

He found a switch. He turned the lights on and almost screamed.

10.

Mister saadi was tied to a chair, smiling horribly. His white teeth shone eerily under the yellow light, among the red splashes which surrounded them. His smile had been enlarged with a razor, which lay at his feet in a puddle of blood. A sign was pinned on his drenched pyjama tops. It was hand-scribbled in red letters, perhaps with the old man's blood, and it read:

"Welcome, mister blind man."

Georg felt dizzy, but he stepped forward and ripped the sign off the dead man's chest while the Special Forces cops brushed past him to check the other rooms.

11.

WHEN SHERYL HUNG up she was shaking like a leaf. She stood silent for a couple of seconds, then picked up the phone again and dialled a number. She felt like she was back ten years ago, and she didn't exactly enjoy the feeling.

12.

Now i can relax—relax and wait for the blind man and his friends—i will soon tell my own story to the scum out there—for nobody else can—and nobody else will

13.

THEY FOUND WHAT they had been looking for in Selim's room. Proofs of his crimes were everywhere. Newspaper articles adorned the four walls, some of them xeroxed up to five times. The victims' belongings crowded his drawers—handbags, make-up, tampons, jewels, everything. They even found their dresses and their shoes in the cupboard, plus the Bible, the Koran and other religious books in the night table. Some of the pages had been scribbled over with obscene drawings; passages had been cut out with scissors. Ratner remembered them pasted on the letters he had received. The room was a mess. But there was no trace of any weapon. And that didn't give Ratner a good feeling at all.

14.

"COMMISSIONER! COMMISSIONER!"

An overweight sergeant hurried towards them as they were walking out of the grocery store.

"Commissioner, there's someone on the phone for you! She says it's important!"

Leaving Valentino and the men, Ratner rushed to the transmission car. Grabbing the receiver from the hands of a puzzled officer, Georg brought it rapidly to his ear.

"Commissioner Ratner speaking...

"Georg, this is Sheryl. Listen, Riban-Riban just called me. He wants to see you and me alone, with a cameraman and some satellite transmission gear; you know what I mean..."

"Where?"

"He didn't say. He told me he would call back in fifteen minutes..."

"Okay, I'll be right over."

"Georg?"

"Yes?"

"I think I'm scared."

"Me too, Sheryl," Ratner said in a lower tone, "me too..."

15.

THE BLIND MAN shall follow her the blonde woman—
and i will meet him and explain—show him the door—the
other door—and then we'll walk through it—together hand in
hand—in the dream of dreams

16.

JESSE WAS DRIVING the car, siren screaming. Ratner hoped they would arrive in time to trace the call. A bleak day was rising through the opening of the avenue. Three police cars followed them, lights flashing. How long until the media would understand that something was taking place? He had given orders to contact the D. A. as late as possible, but leaks were still possible.

"I think it's time to quote a poem," Jesse said.

Ratner listened to him distractedly.

Poetry, yeah.

That was all they had left now.

17.

ONE OF THE things that bothered the Commissioner was how Selim had learned he had discovered the truth. Coincidence? He shivered in his seat, and his hand searched mechanically for a cigar. There was another explanation, but he wasn't crazy enough yet to believe in it. He preferred to cling to the first idea. Coincidence.

18.

THE LABYRINTH HAS many corridors Georg Ratner and many chambers—and sometimes you know where you are and sometimes you don't—even if you think you do—believe me—i know

19.

Sheryl opened to the cops and ran into Georg's arms.

The Commissioner gently pushed her back.

"Has he called again?"

The phone rang the second she was shaking her head. Georg motioned to the transmission officers who rushed in with their strange equipment. He took Sheryl by the arm and walked with her to the dining room. When the policemen were ready, he nodded to Sheryl to pick up the phone. He noticed she was sweating. Then again, so was he.

Riban-Riban's voice crackled through the room.

Joyce, who had just walked in with fresh coffee for the police team, froze on the spot.

The voice was sweet, much too sweet—and twisted.

It curved, looped, and dropped.

Ratner listened with attention, although he could feel his stomach turning.

It was a love declaration.

A sick, dark and passionate love declaration to religion, the world and... Georg Ratner.

"I love the blind man; I want him. Everyday I want him. And I want the television to show it. Show my love. You understand? Women, they lie to me. It's not their fault, but they lie. Even you, you lie. It's not your fault. But I know. I know everything."

Sheryl was trembling and Ratner had closed his eyes.

"The blind man he comes to me at night, and I can see his yellow skin. I can almost touch him everyday, but he doesn't see me. Never. Dark sunglasses for the blind man. Now, I know, he can see. And we shall meet soon, and you will show the people our love. For he loves me. We are the same."

Jesse Valentino was clutching his hands together.

Minutes passed. The tracing machines were emitting strange sounds. The cops fiddled with buttons.

Riban–Riban finally said where they should meet.

"At the old bridge. In twenty minutes. I have a hostage."

"Shit!" one of the policemen said.

This summed up the situation perfectly, Ratner thought to himself. Couldn't have found a better word.

20.

THE OLD BRIDGE was located in the western suburb of the city, an old industrial area now plagued with chemical poisons. It was entirely in the hands of street gangs, and various violent insurrection movements. Police very seldom went there, and the Mayor had almost declared the zone "autonomous." If they had sent a major police force, this would have been interpreted as "police provocation," and would have no doubt triggered a series of major incidents, something neither the Mayor, nor the D. A. would appreciate, with the upcoming elections. Not that Ratner cared, really, but the life of his men mattered to him, and going there would certainly put them in jeopardy. The risk was too great for the reward. A single murderer, famous now as he was, didn't deserve the life of his best men. He thought rapidly about the situation and turned to Valentino.

"I'm sorry to ask you this, but do you know how to work a video camera?"

21.

IN THE BUS BTV had lent them for the special operation they were all silent. Georg was at the wheel, chewing an unlit cigar. Sheryl was looking out the window and, in the back, Lieutenant Valentino was reading the directions for the portable video camera he was going to use in a moment.

"Shit, Georg," Sheryl finally sighed, "I'm getting too old for this..."

Ratner grunted.

"Someone's got to do it."

She smiled sadly.

"What will they write on our graves?"

Ratner shrugged, his eyes still on the road. They were almost there now.

"I don't know. Probably something like *If only they had known better...*"

They laughed briefly, but the bridge suddenly appeared after the corner of a desolate, burned-down block, and silence fell again.

22.

SHERYL GOT OUT of the van first and pulled at her dress. Valentino followed her while Ratner checked the bullets in his gun. Satisfied, he put it back in the pocket of his coat.

The freezing wind caught his breath as soon as he stepped out. The two others had been waiting for him and they began their walk towards the eerie ruin, which gleamed sadly in the new day rising.

23.

"STAY RIGHT THERE or I fuck her up!"

The trio stopped some thirty feet away, obeying the assassin's order. He was holding a naked woman by the hair and had a small hand axe hovering over her head.

"So you've come, finally!" he shouted in the mild breeze. "I was getting worried. Is that the special camera for satellite transmission?"

Sheryl shouted back that it was.

"Very good! You have a zoom lense, don't you?"

Sheryl confirmed again.

"Excellent! So you can stay where you are! And don't try to get any closer, because otherwise..."

He shook the hand which held the axe. They all got the message.

"You can start filming now. I've got a little TV set right here, so I can see if you're really transmitting..."

"The bastard," Sheryl mumbled.

"Do what he says," Ratner said. "I need time to think."

Sheryl nodded and Valentino set the camera on his shoulder. She grabbed the microphone.

"This is Sheryl Boncoeur, coming to you live from City West..."

24.

RATNER WALKED CAUTIOUSLY to the bridge, squeezing the gun in his pocket. All of this was so pathetic, so out of measure... a *grande finale* for a pathetic moron. He thought about all the other morons, glued to their TV screens at this very moment, waiting for something to happen, something fun... But what scared him even more was what was going to happen afterwards, when all of this would be finished.

25.

"THIS IS SHERYL BONCOEUR, live from the Old Bridge...The Commissioner is now almost at the bridge...Yes, he's arriving now...The criminal is still threatening the woman, who seems to have lost consciousness... It's very difficult to see anything from here... Jesse, maybe you could make a close-up..."

26.

RATNER COULD SEE Selim perfectly clear now. The young man was wearing two pairs of sunglasses on his nose, which gave him a eerie clownish look. The woman he was threatening had passed out, blue with cold. Hypothermia, he thought. The young assassin smiled and let go of the woman's hair as Georg walked closer. He didn't seem frightened at all. In fact, he almost looked friendly.

"Ah, Commissioner, we meet at last..."

His voice sounded strange, echoing at the same time from the portable TV set he had installed on the bridge.

"Doesn't all this look a little familiar? I remember you very well from the dream. You were wearing the same clothes, but it was much hotter... Could we have met in hell, tell me? It wasn't clear in the dream... But the bull was... And, by Allah, what a bull it—"

The detonation startled even the Commissioner, and Riban-Riban flew backwards, spraying thousands of little red dots over the girl's blue body. Ratner kept on shooting through the pocket of his coat, again and again, until all six bullets were securely lodged inside the motionless corpse. Then he softly untied the woman's hands, which fell like two lumps of cold meat on the ground.

27.

"You could have waited a little longer," Sheryl said later, as the ambulances were driving away. "It was getting quite interesting..."

Georg looked at her beautiful blue eyes and smiled distantly.

"Shut the fuck up, Sheryl, okay? Just shut the fuck up."

28.

THINGS WENT AS he had feared.

The mayor wanted to see him and congratulate him. The D. A. wanted to see him and congratulate him. He just felt tired. He wanted a vacation, retirement, or both.

Jesse was driving.

"What did you think of my filming?" he asked the Commissioner.

Ratner sighed.

"What did you think of my shooting?"

He thought he had been ironic enough, but the Lieutenant missed the point.

"It was perfect shooting, Chief. It looked great on TV!"

Ratner sighed again, deeper this time.

There was no hope in this fucking life.

Not even in dreams.

29.

DREAMS.

He had been stupid to believe in them. They were as shitty as the rest. A mirror of the world. Noût, Goddess of prostitutes. Crazy yellow bulls roaming around, red foam at the mouth. All paths went in but one direction: more paths. They crossed, they went in parallel lines, but they drew the same crazy labyrinth. There was no exit

and no entrance. You were just born in it. When Theseus removed the mask of the Minotaur, he probably saw his own face, and went insane. *Glasses for the blind man*—a verse in one of Riban-Riban's letters. Selim had been right, somehow. We were all lost in the same room. Jesse was whistling, his two hands on the steering wheel.

"Hey, Jesse, do you believe in dreams?"

Jesse briefly turned his head around.

"Didn't we have this talk before, Chief?"

Ratner nodded, lighting a cigar.

"Yes, we did..."

What had Noût said in his dream again?

Ah yes: "There is only life."

Life.

That was it.

The labyrinth.

30.

THE MAYOR MADE a little speech at the town hall while flashes crackled all around. He shook the hands of Georg, Sheryl and Jesse, thanking them again for their "outstanding courage." Questions were asked from all sides, and Ratner let Sheryl do most of the talking. Jesse smiled brightly and his face was flushed with pride. He would probably soon be promoted Captain, which would make him the youngest of this city, just like Georg had been, some years ago.

The D. A. joined the celebration and gave a little speech in his turn. You would never have thought the elections were coming in three weeks. Everybody loved everybody. The city could breathe. The terrible assassin had been shot by the courageous Commissioner.

Music, please.

Sheryl suddenly grabbed Ratner's arm. He turned around, surprised. She handed him a glass of champagne and took him aside in a corner, away from the general commotion.

"I want to apologize," she said.

He raised a weary eyebrow.

"For what I said, about not waiting long enough when you shot that bastard... I don't know what got into me... You know what they say: "Once a shark, always a shark," and yes, I admit, I could smell blood... Only, this time, it could have been yours..."

He took a sip of his glass and smiled.

"It's okay, Sheryl, it's okay...You're a professional, that's all. A true professional—whatever that means..."

She smiled back, and they raised their glasses.

31.

THE D. A. LOOKED at him with surprise.

"A vacation? Now?"

Georg looked across the crowded room where the reception was still going strong.

"It's either that or I grab any reporter in this room and tell him I am resigning for good."

The D. A. had a nervous smile.

"You wouldn't do this to me three weeks before the elections, would you?"

Georg smiled back.

"Try me."

The D. A. put his glass down and wiped the sweat off his neck with a white handkerchief.

"I'll give you two weeks, if you can wait after the elections."

Georg pretended to think about it.

"Five weeks."

The little man nervously scratched his balding head.

"This city can't go without you for more than three weeks, Georg! Especially not if I appoint you... Commissioner-in-Chief..."

The word lingered for a few seconds, but Georg laughed.

"You're going to do that anyway. You have to. I know that and you know that. I don't give a damn about this, you know that too. Five weeks. I need five weeks. No more, no less, or I quit for good. Take it or leave it. All I need to do is to go talk to Sheryl Boncoeur and—

"—All right, all right. Five weeks. But after the elections, uh?"

Georg nodded, and brought the glass to his lips.

32.

HE TOOK A cab to go to the hospital. He was too tired to drive. It was almost noon now, and the sky was clearing. Patches of blue ripped through the grey clouds.

"Looks like we're in it for some better weather," the cabdriver said.

Georg agreed and looked out of the dirty window. The sun could shine if it wanted to. It wouldn't change a thing in this goddamned city. Not a single thing. People needed to believe in things like better weather to keep going. Something. Anything. The sun. Good weather. Birds singing. Television games. Soap operas. Whatever—and maybe it was for the best, after all. We couldn't go on suffering all our life, could we? He shifted position and smiled a very thin smile, pressing his forehead against the cold glass. Or—could we?

33.

THE NURSE BARELY looked at him when he signed the book. It was good to know that some things never changed.

34.

THE BODY OF his wife lay still in the half-light. The curtains had been drawn, and he had often wondered why, as Barbara could not see anything, anyway. Maybe it was for dramatic effect. He sat down next to her and took her hand. She was still smiling at the ceiling, and he felt somewhat jealous.

Stroking her fingers, his thoughts drifted to the past days.

"There is only life," the Goddess had said.

"A labyrinth," Selim had assessed.

He brought the fingers to his lips and kissed them. They smelled of medicinal soap. It wasn't her smell. It was the hospital's smell. He suddenly felt angry. They were trying to remove her from him, to lock her in this room, like a treasure in a safe...

He looked at all the screens of the machines, the tubes, the dials... He had thought about switching them off many times, but he never had had the courage, not even last night, with the syringe he had stolen, and which was still in the pocket of his coat. It could be so simple now, a bubble of air in the tubes, and no more labyrinths... He shook his head and stroked her beautiful hair.

How could he think about such things?

He was not revolted, just curious. The yellow bull had stared at him in his dream and Selim had seen it, but even if they had somehow shared the same dream, they hadn't seen the same thing. A thousand doors and a thousand rooms. There was no choice, because it was *impossible* to choose. Selim thought he could open the right door and he had chosen the one which was labelled "Destruction," but destruction was not the answer—and neither was construction.

Hesitation, maybe.

Yes, he liked that word, "hesitation." It had a nice ring to it. The ring of truth.

He ran a finger along her well-drawn eyebrows.

He had done this a lot of times before the accident.

He was in love with her eyebrows.

Bridges over her eyes, he used to say.

"I love you," he whispered in her empty ear. "I will never forget you."

The machines made a strange purring sound, drawing his attention. He was linked to the machines too, and so was Laura. They were all attached to the wires and dials, to the semi-obscurity of the room, like trees to their deepest roots. There was no point in trying to escape. Even death would not free any of them. Death cannot free life. It is not in its attributions.

Riban-Riban had misunderstood that, and so had the world. They had all believed that if you could control one, you had power over the other. Bullshit. Death was death and life was life. There were no connections between the two of them. They were both mysteries, forming the walls of this goddamned labyrinth, with no exit and no entrance.

He bent over to kiss her lips, something he hadn't done since he had met Laura. They were warm and he kissed them again. Noût had been right: one path did not necessarily exclude another. There was only life, and life was an eternal contradiction.

35.

BEFORE LEAVING, HE broke the unused syringe in two and dropped it into the garbage can, where it landed with a little "clang!"

The sound of peace and relief.

36.

IN THE HALL of the hospital, he went to make a phone call.

He left a message on Laura's answering machine, inviting her to his apartment later that evening. He called his office afterwards and said he would be gone all afternoon.

A long line of taxis were parked in front of the building. He climbed into one and told the driver to take him downtown. He knew a travel agency on 71st Avenue where he could get good deals on flights. There was about half an hour ride to the

center of the city and Ratner settled more comfortably in the backseat. It was about time he saw those goddamned pyramids, and he was sure Laura could use a vacation too. His eyelids began to close and as his head dropped on his chest, he wished his sleep would be pitch-black, deep and, above all, dreamless.

THE GARDENS
OF BABYLON

To François Bouët-Willaumez,
with all my love and everything that goes with it.

"This subject is riddled with parasites."

William S. Burroughs

DEATH

Sitting on the toilet bowl, Speedy Jimmy, a.k.a. "Jimmy Quick Death," a.k.a "Too Late Jimmy," was once again reading the back cover of the stupid book, his jaws clenched with rage. It was a poor quality paperback edition of THE SECRET LIFE OF SPEEDY JIMMY, typical of the New Babylonian Press recent releases, with a cheap blurry black-and-white photograph of the author—Old Bulldog himself—smiling his eternal rattlesnake smile. Jimmy sneezed and wiped his nose with a piece of toilet paper. His nose kept tingling, but he didn't care. He viciously cleared his throat and spit between his knees.

What had got into the old fruit?

They had been friends in the past—close friends, to say the least.

Jimmy could still remember when he had first arrived in Babylon, with no money inside his pierced pockets, and how Bulldog—a friend of his late father, but still—had immediately hired him in his famous Poet-Assassin Guild. Bulldog, a writer himself and a lover of firearms, had organized a gang of for-hire murderers consisting of aspiring poets and novelists who, as payment for their assignments, had the privilege of being published in one of the numerous New Babylonian Press collections, a company partly owned, of course, by Old Bulldog himself.

In these difficult times, many authors applied but only the best shots were chosen. It was a great privilege, as the Guild rated the highest among the murder companies and first-hand accounts of cold-blooded paid-for assassinations were always number one bestsellers, as were what were called the "Death Poetry Collections."

Jimmy told himself that his father had been right to teach him how to shoot when he was five—this had sure proved useful. Too bad little Jimmy also had to be his favorite moving target...

It sure had been an incredible opportunity for the then-young Jimmy to have been hired by the Bull. He had killed his way to the top in an astoundingly short amount of time, building himself a well-deserved reputation along the way. Such a good reputation, in fact, that he had chosen to go freelance after only a few years, something Old Bull had never quite forgiven him, and which probably explained the origins of the book... And what a book!

The Bull was going to pay for this piece of crap, no doubt, but there was still one little problem: the contract...

Murder was legal in Babylon, as long as you had a valid contract and were registered with one of the 57 official Assassin Compagnies that existed in the city. The authorities had taken the measure in order to control the ever-growing crime scene, and it was a good way to balance the budget, as all killing contracts were heavily taxed.

Jimmy scratched his chin, his eyes lost in the distance.

One of his legs was getting tired, and he shook it for a little while, wincing.

The itch was that nobody would put forth a contract on the Bull. Nobody. Like himself now, Bulldog was too famous a character—some smart-ass journalist had even called him an "institution." Oh, there had been attempts all right: angered members of some victims' family, other Guilds jealous of Bull's successes, disgruntled lovers... All of them bloody failures.

Old Bull was still alive and doing well. Since the last attempt, though, he had moved to a safer place, the address of which was kept secret.

Jimmy furrowed his brow, in dark thoughts.

To kill someone without a proper contract was a very, very

risky business: if you got caught, it meant endless years in prison, or worse—exile for life.

Jimmy knew he couldn't live anywhere else but in this city. He had made it his. He had turned it into his own personal garden, hunting ground, leisure park, all that... And where else could he go?

Jerusalem? Murderers were not welcome there.

Saint Petersburg? He came from there; better not think about it.

Paris, London, Kyoto? Sissy cities.

No, it was Babylon, once and for all.

The Bull deserved to be punished, though. He had turned his life into a nightmare with his book. Even Belle had asked him if it was true that he had slept with Old Bulldog in order to get the job. His own wife, figure that! There it was, page 56: "Getting down on his knees, Jimmy gave me the best blow-job ever..."

He finally got up from the seat, angrily wiped himself, flushed the toilet and walked out. The book lay at the feet of the porcelain bowl, forgotten and fat and black like a dirty toad.

DOPE

Cassandra woke up and wished she hadn't.

The empty space next to her in the bed was like a black, heavy, magnetic vortex dragging her towards its center.

She missed him. God, she did.

She sat up, feeling sick and dizzy. The room was a mess. Her clothes were spread all over the floor, most of them unwashed; piles of dishes crowded the sink, sheets of paper were scattered everywhere, but she didn't care anymore. Sal was gone now, leaving her behind like the coward, the jerk, the asshole he had always been—and yes, she did miss him, nonetheless—but enough of that.

She decided it was time to get up, and she did. Her legs were long and white out of the covers: some said beautiful, she preferred skinny.

Shivering, she heated some water for coffee. Waiting for the unnerving whistle of the boiler, she rummaged in her handbag, her eyes concentrated like two tiny green spots. There it was, finally: half a dose.

Shit. She suddenly felt like crying.

Half a fucking dose! It wasn't anywhere close enough. She would have to call Marty soon. Real soon. That bastard. She hated him, but the water was whining now, and so were her body cells, craving for the stuff in the little cellophane bags, the stuff that was 10.000 times better than coffee—and coffee could wait.

DEATH

The sun was rising over Babylon, and from the bay windows of the apartment the view was superb. The sun was now peeking through the gap between the Gandhi Towers, setting the roofs on fire. The light shuffle of footsteps made him turn around. Belle was still wrapped in her transparent nightgown, holding a book in her hand. Jimmy could see it was The Gardens of Babylon, the recent illegal bestseller everybody was—cautiously—talking about.

Any book rejected by the official New Babylonian Press was declared "illegal," and it was therefore absolutely forbidden to anyone to read, distribute or publish it. A few underground presses still resisted, however, such as the Babylonian Revolutionary Press, which had published the infamous bestseller.

The Gardens of Babylon, whose author went by the pseudonym of "Al Alamein," was a long, beautiful, twisted love story between a pair of Siamese twins and two dwarf sisters. Although it bore no particular political allusions and was set in mythical times, the New Babylonian Press committee of readers had considered its style subversive and harmful for civil peace. It had consequently outlawed the book and its author, offering a substantial reward to anyone who could give any kind of information leading to the arrest of the infamous "Al Alamein."

Jimmy, through business connections, had managed to obtain a copy of the book and had read it several times already.

He had acquired a taste for good literature while he was still working for the Guild, in reaction to what his colleagues published in the New Babylonian Press collections. At the time, he had written a few collections of poetry, one of which, Stains like Red Stars, had met with critical esteem and a certain amount of sale success. Old Bull himself had written the foreword to the fourth edition, may he burn in hell.

"A beautiful day, isn't it?" Belle whispered in his ear.

He shivered and smiled, holding her in his arms.

"Do you still love me?" she asked, biting the lobe of his ear.

As she pressed herself against him he felt the sharp corner of the book sink into the muscles of his back, like a lethal, but friendly, weapon.

POETRY

Sitting in front of his cup of coffee, Stefan Marcovitch, a.k.a. "Al Alamein," a.k.a. "Wanted for illegal and subversive writing, etc., etc., etc.," reread the letter for the seventh time:

Dear Sir,

We have come across your novel, The Gardens of Babylon—through non-official channels, of course, as you surely understand¾and we have been quite impressed with its uncommon qualities. We have our reasons to believe that your book is promised to a great literary future, and yourself to a fine career in our city, where, as you probably know already, publishing laws are somewhat different than there, to say the least.

We are thus offering you political and literary asylum in Saint Petersburg, as well as the immediate and official publication of your book. You will find a plane ticket, money and everything you need in order to safely get to Saint Petersburg enclosed in this letter, as well as directions useful upon your arrival.

Sincerely hoping to see you soon. Yours truly,

Søren Johannesen

YELLOW ROSE PRESS

Saint Petersburg

The letter had been slipped under his door, unstamped and unmarked. It contained a plane ticket, a foreign credit card and a fake passport. Stefan Marcovitch folded the letter back into the envelope and took a deep breath.

This letter was a miracle.

He smiled to himself and shook his head.

He didn't believe in miracles, though. Or rather, coffee was the only miracle he still believed in. He took a sip and burned his tongue.

DEATH

Breakfast was over.

Jimmy got up as the maid, a large Ethiopian woman who never said a word, began to clear the table. In the corridor, he could hear Belle sing under the shower. She had the voice of a siren, and if he had been Ulysses, he would have untied himself and jumped into the lethal waters to meet her.

Smiling—the loving feelings he had for his wife always put him in a good mood—he walked into his office, closing the door behind him. He picked up the thick leather-bound agenda resting on his desk and flipped through the pages until he found the one he was looking for.

> JUNE 1st Saint Justin. 256-302. First bishop of
> the Bulgarian church, martyred by the Scythes
> in Zadar.
> Sunrise 5:37 AM.
> Sunset 8:48 PM.
> Quote of the day:"Bald men make better soldiers,"
> Sun Ya-tsen.

There was a name written in red under this: "Sheryl Boncoeur"—the famous TV critic.

"Easy," Jimmy thought with a smile.

A perfect job for a Sunday.

He put the agenda down and let his eyes wander through

the window. There were thin trails of smoke rising over the skyline, like the white columns of an industrial temple. The image pleased him. Ah, poetry. Maybe someday he would go back to his old flame and pick up the pen again. A sharp knock on the door cut short his sentimental daydreaming.

"Darling, it's me!" Belle said from behind the door.

He told her to come in and she appeared in the doorway, barely covered by a wet towel, radiant in the sunlight. She was holding another book in her hand.

"I found this in the bathroom," she said, with a slight hesitation in her voice. "What should I do with it?"

He looked at The Secret Life of Speedy Jimmy and felt a wave of blind rage storm through his soul. Old Bull's disgusting bundle of lies slowly began to burn inside his head, burn until there was nothing left but a little pile of ashes, scattered away by the sweet breeze of vengeance.

DOPE

Cassandra slowly extracted the needle from her vein and untied the rubber

band squeezing her arm. A fat drop of blood squirted out from the tiny hole and ran down the pale skin of her arm to the tip of her fingers. Her eyes became vague and a faint smile appeared on her tired face.

When she was a little girl, not so many years ago, she lived in a white house in the countryside and she was happy there, she remembered, until some things happened and she had to move to the city. But that was okay because she had dreamt so many times about it...

and then, some other things happened and some didn't, and she had met him one evening in a bar, like most people do, yes, him, Sal, and Sal had told her about things in poems he had written for her, only for her

and Sal would call her his muse, that's right, his muse, whatever that meant, and she accepted it because she loved him, and he needed her love, at least that was what he used to say

so she had been his muse until he had died, three weeks ago, she had found him all blue in the face with fried-yellow eyes and foam at the mouth, "an overdose" had said the paramedic, that was it, no sad music, no white stairs, no angels, just the closing of the door and the wailing of sirens

and they had left her all alone to pick up the pieces of

this crazy puzzle, with all his words scattered on papers, empty words now, flat, black and white lines scattered everywhere on the table, under the bed, above the fridge, on the walls, pinned like the absurd maps of his desolation and madness, so many words, so many useless words...

so much paper with no good purpose

so many lines and so many lies

and maybe she should gather them all and burn them up, burn it all

burn what was left of him

and her

DEATH

Speedy Jimmy looked at himself in the standing mirror of the hallway, turning around and arranging his hair. He looked good. The heavy eight-round Tokarev hung coolly under his left arm, throwing its reassuring shadow across the white T-shirt.

"You look good," Belle confirmed and kissed him.

They looked at their own reflection in the silver glass. The assassin and his loving wife. He had met her during one of his assignments, three years ago. She was the secretary of a rock'n'roll manager he had a contract on. She had let him in the victim's office with a strange smile, as if she had guessed what he had come for. This had struck him, he could still remember, as well as her piercing blue eyes. The job finished and the unfortunate manager left to stare at his ten thousand dollar Turkish rug forever, he had asked her out and she had immediately accepted.

"Now that I'm free and without a job," she had said, gathering her purse and coat, "I can do whatever you want..."

They had gotten married three weeks later.

He grabbed the heavy leather jacket hanging from the coat hanger, as well as his motorcycle helmet.

"I'll be home around six," he said. "Then we'll go out for dinner."

She nodded and they kissed again.

"Be a good girl," he added, walking out the door.

He loved her very much. Almost as much as killing.

DOPE

The whirling kaleidoscope finally stopped spinning and became her room again¾small, dirty and empty. Staring around, Cassandra realized that nothing could ever fill the void Sal had left behind, not even the ashes of his entire life. A violent kick of her stomach reminded her that she couldn't just sit and grope all day. She had to call Marty, and this couldn't wait. She also had a shift at the Sonic at nine, and she needed the money badly.

One of Sal's poems was sticking out from under the bed.

She picked it up and held it to the light. It read: Rock'n'roll is killing my life.

Ditto.

She crumpled it into a ball and turned the radio on.

She picked up the receiver and dialled Marty's number. Magnetic voices and music mingled with hers as she began to speak.

POETRY

The streets were almost empty, like on all Sunday mornings. Stefan liked the feeling of walking alone in the big city. Taking a deep breath, he inhaled the mixed smells floating around—car fumes, newspaper ink, dog shit, saturated ozone, cheap perfume, all these—a poem to come, the first lines of a novel, a story in itself... Reaching in his jacket, he felt the letter under his fingers.

Saint Petersburg.

Next chapter?

Maybe...

"Stefan!"

He turned around and was blinded by the sun. A tall, dark silhouette was strolling towards him, handbag spinning in her hand.

"Hi, Louise."

The woman stopped a few inches away from him, too close for comfort. Stefan felt a strange tingling in his toes.

"You're working, already?" he asked her, trying to sound cool and detached, but his voice croaked a bit anyway.

She was like a huge magnet in a car cemetery.

She was a cold sun shining high over his head.

She was his muse.

His secret inspiration.

She never let him pay.

She said she liked him.

Words always got caught in his throat when he wanted to speak to her. So he had to make love to her, and write.

She shrugged and shook her beautiful blonde hair.

"The kid is sick. I need some money to buy some medicine."

Stefan nodded, looking at an imaginary spot above her left shoulder. She was too beautiful for such an early hour in the morning. Sometimes he wondered if he was in love with her, but never for too long, because it was not safe to ask yourself these kinds of questions, especially not about a prostitute.

He had to walk away.

He felt like running.

He told her he had something very important to do and had to be on his way.

She smiled, ignoring the lie, and kissed him gently on the lips.

"I'll be here tonight if you need me!" she shouted as he disappeared at the corner of the street. "I'll be waiting for you!"

Stefan pressed on, not looking back.

The letter in his pocket weighed a ton.

DEATH

The 1200 cc "Indian Chief" motorcycle was waiting for Jimmy on the sidewalk, gleaming quietly like a sleeping dragon.

DOPE

The park was crowded with children.

Their screams and laughter filled the air like music. The mothers chatted around, sitting on benches. The sky was deep blue and a few clouds hung here and there, white like dope.

Cassandra looked at her watch.

She hoped Marty wouldn't be too late.

POETRY

Louise is
a bird on the tramway wires
that sings something you can't hear
because of the cars below

Louise is
a cloud
light and white
slowly pushed away
by the wind

Louise is
a woman in a short dress
as pure and holy
as we are not

Louise is
a woman and a whore
and much much more
she is a city
     the city
         this city
unique Miss Louise Babylon
heartbreak of them all
including me
oh yeah
including me

DEATH

The sun was reflected on the water, making it shine like metal. The rays pierced Jimmy's eyes behind the goggles. He gave a little more gas, feeling the engine shake and rumble between his thighs. Adrenalin shot down his spine, reaching the tip of his fingers like ice-cold water.

The bridge stood in front of him, linking the two sides of the city like a gigantic stitch, offering its back to the bike's wheels like some helpful servant, sodomite lover... The words reminded him of Old Bull and his hands tightened around the handlebars.

"Soon," he told himself, grinding his teeth, "soon."

POETRY

Stefan was walking for the last time in the streets of the city that had been the source of his inspiration. It struck him suddenly. Yes, for the last time...

The situation gave him no choice, really: Saint Petersburg or twelve years in prison. This was the tariff. Maybe nine, with a sympathetic judge.   He walked into a store and bought a quart of whisky.

He would wander about the streets today, then, and maybe write something along the way, something that would remind him later of Babylon, and make him want to come back.

DOPE

The gardens were the pride of the city. They spread for a mile and a half through its center, a puddle of green in a sea of grey. It was the meeting point for mothers, lovers, doomsday preachers and—last but not the least—junkies.

A whole area, known as the White Zone, was their turf, and the police had given up the idea of cleaning it up years ago. It was actually still a very beautiful place, sheltered by trees, hills and flower bushes, surrounding the large round artificial lake.

A regular biochemical garden of Eden.

Cassandra picked up a handful of pebbles and threw them one by one into the water, watching her own reflection break up and disappear, again and again.

DEATH

Sheryl Boncoeur lived in a luxurious mansion overlooking the river, located in the best part of town. The area was beautiful and quiet, with trim-cut lawns and electronically protected entrances. There were less and less pedestrians, Jimmy noticed as he rode by, and more and more foreign cars. He finally stopped in front of a flower shop in Boncoeur's street and he bought a dozen white roses—most of these stores were open on Sundays because of parties and funerals.

"The lady will surely appreciate," said the fleuriste, a little fat Chinese woman with too much makeup.

"I'm sure she will," agreed the young assassin, flashing one of his most charming smiles.

DOPE

Marty wasn't too late, for once. He displayed a golden tan, as if he spent all his week-ends at the beach, which he probably did, as a matter of fact.

"Hey, baby, what's up?" he enquired, excessively good-humored as usual.

Cassandra was feeling cold lightning bolts shoot up and down her arms and legs at the speed of light.

"You know what's up... I've got the money..."

"Let me see..."

He took the crumpled bills from her shaky hand and proceeded to count. When he had finished, he shook his head with a sad grin on his face and she felt her heart drop.

"Sorry, honey, but that's far from enough."

A wave of panic seized her.

"But last time, it was... it was..."

"Last time was last time, sugar. Today, it's more. Times are hard, prices are going up. You don't know what I've got to go through to please all of you goddamned people..."

She grabbed his arm, squeezing it frantically.

"Please! Please, help me! You've got to! You've got to!"

Frowning, he seemed to be thinking for a minute, then a smile flashed on his face.

"Okay," he finally said, "I've got an idea."

He slowly lifted her T-shirt and groped one of her breasts

with his hard hand. She thought of a warm spider and tried to restrain the sickness and tears overwhelming her.

"I've got a great idea," he repeated, dragging her towards the dark bushes.

Trees circles over their heads like silent voyeurs. The spider crawled under her skirt.

POETRY

In the bus, Stefan sat in front of a very cute girl with a slightly hooked nose. He watched the city streets roll through the dirty windows like a sad German movie. From the corner of his eye, he could see that the girl was watching him and thought of a beautiful story to write. The girl finally got up and left, leaving the seat empty for more inspiration.

DEATH

Boncoeur's butler, a very dignified old Arab wearing a fez for authenticity purposes, no doubt, carefully looked at Jimmy, one of his eyebrows slightly raised in surprise.

"Flowers from a secret admirer," Jimmy explained with a wink. "Special delivery..."

And God knew that was true.

POETRY

Stefan got off the bus and took a few steps on the asphalt.

The harbor lay in front of him, spreading its fish-smelling arms. A few ships were sleeping along the wharfs, like huge rust mountains brought in by the sea.

He had always loved the harbor.

The proximity of adventure.

The strange names of the ships.

The containers and their mysterious contents.

Saint Petersburg only had a military port.

Raising the quart high in the air, he took a swig and began to cough under the amused eyes of two sailors running to catch their ship.

DEATH

The butler rapped on the door and walked in. Sitting behind a large ebony desk, Sheryl Boncoeur raised her eyes from the papers she was reading. She looked much older than he thought.

"This is the gentleman with the flowers, miss," the old servant announced.

"Very well, Ali, you may leave us now."

The servant let Jimmy in and shut the door behind him. Boncoeur went back to her papers.

"Ali told me these flowers were sent to me by some secret admirer... May I ask who it is?"

Jimmy took a few steps in the office. He could see Boncoeur's grey hair bob up and down as the famous journalist read the various documents scattered under her nose. He quietly moved closer.

"Well, you know miss, if it's a secret, it's a secret..."

"True, but too bad," the critic agreed, writing something down in the margin of a yellow page.

Jimmy's knees were now touching the desk.

"I have, however, this note for you..." Jimmy quickly added, putting his hand in his jacket.

Boncoeur finally looked up, only to find the muzzle of the Tokarev hovering a few inches above her nose.

"What the..." she growled, but Jimmy fired once, sending the journalist flying backwards against her armchair.

Blood had sprayed on the bouquet of roses, shining on the petals like tiny red pearls.

"Such a poet, I am," thought Jimmy, firing a second shot, just to make sure.

He was a professional, after all.

POETRY

A drunken sailor with a tattoo on his arm
dances with an imaginary siren
—the tattoo is blue and so is the sea
spelling one of the 1000 names of despair
Sailor! Sailor! So happy to come home
and yet impatient to leave again
to other harbors and other names
—memories are nothing but tattoos and the smell
of cheap alcohol and sometimes, sometimes a face
but it always changes and is never the same

DEATH

Jimmy arranged the roses around Sheryl Boncoeur's body, so that the place wouldn't look too messy. He had always cherished neat killings and was only half-pleased with this one. He shouldn't have fired from such a short distance... Next time he would be more careful.

He left his card on the desk, along with a copy of the contract, for the police records. As he closed the door behind him it suddenly occurred to him that he used to really enjoy reading Boncoeur's columns in the Babylonian Star. She was one of the few honest voices left around.

"The best ones are always the first ones to go..." he muttered to himself, shaking his head. "Just like my mamma used to say: Sic transit gloria mundi."

DOPE

From the open window of the public toilet she could hear the children screaming and laughing. Two little bags were scattered around the stained sink, one of them already half empty.

The bastard had been generous.

The needle was vanilla ice cream cold in her forearm.

A river of gold and silver began to run in her veins.

The Eldorado.

The toilet seat became a velvet throne.

Urine smelled of incense.

Marty's spunk had dried out and fallen out of her womb like tiny white rocks into the sea. Nothing was left of him. Not a trace.

Tears began to roll down her cheeks.

Outside, the children were still screaming, but louder.

POETRY

Stefan remained on the bench facing the pier for a little while. The empty bottle lay at his feet like a useless companion. A Russian cargo ship entered the harbor, huge and covered with rust. He slowly got to his feet.

It was time to leave.

The horizon was blocked.

DEATH

Jimmy stopped for lunch at a Scandinavian fast-food. Munching on a shrimps and caviar sandwich, he wondered who could give him Bulldog's new address. As he had no contract, there was no point in asking his sources inside the police department.

No, he had to find someone safe.

Someone he could rely on.

His face suddenly lit up and he stopped chewing for a second.

Of course, he knew someone—and he wondered why he hadn't thought about him earlier...

DOPE

In the bus on her way to the Sonic Bar, Cassandra looked at the streets of the city through the large dusty windows. They formed a labyrinth of concrete and dirt with a Minotaur at every corner, waiting to feed on fresh meat.

But she was no Ariadne herself—no sir, not at all.

She was like all the others: she was lost in this labyrinth too.

DEATH

The bouncer looked at Jimmy over the book he was reading and spat a few inches away from his boots.

"Long time no see," he said, shaking the assassin's hand.

There was already a line in front of the Sonic Bar, although this was a Sunday and early afternoon, but it was a legendary joint after all—the first of its kind, mixing booze, strippers and all kinds of violent music—and Juan Speck, its more than successful owner, happened to be a long-time friend of Jimmy's.

Speck was a retired killer himself and the secret editor of the Babylonian Revolutionary Press. The bar was a cover for his illegal activities and a seemingly never-ending source of finance. Speck also happened to be Old Bull's most notorious enemy—a story dating back to the times when the New Babylonian Press had rejected his first novel, although he was still officially working for the Poet-Assassin Guild. The rejection slip had stated that the work was "too extreme" for any of their existing collections...

Speck had never forgiven Bulldog for this and had later started his own underground publishing company, swearing to bring the NBP down to its knees through parallel competition.

"I can see some things don't change," Jimmy said, pointing at the crowd waiting outside.

"Unfortunately," the bouncer agreed, letting him in despite loud protests coming from a cluster of over made-up teenage girls.

"You shut up now," growled the giant, "or you never get in, okay?"

The argument sounded powerful enough and silence fell again in the line.

Jimmy winked as he passed the doorway. The bouncer winked back and buried his nose into his book again.

POETRY

Stefan Marcovitch strolled for hours in the quiet city. Fragments of poems and stories sometimes surprised him around the corners, but he left them behind as he walked on. He didn't want anymore poems, anymore stories. He wanted a peaceful, innocent and harmless goodbye, but it was so hard: there are no innocent words when you were about to leave your mistress.

DOPE

Nathan, the bouncer, bent over to kiss her cheek.

Funny how a giant could be so delicate. It always surprised her, although she had been working at the Sonic for a little over a year now.

Nathan raised his huge body again, straightened his pants and pointed at the line with his large thumb.

"It's really busy today… Good luck!"

She smiled.

"Thanks, I'll need it!"

And boy, he didn't know how much she needed it.

POETRY

He walked through the park, the world-famous Gardens of Babylon, where kids played and junkies died, like his friend Sal, a poet too, another lost soul and all that.

A shooting star, literally.

Stefan used to envy him a lot, when Sal was still alive. He had a special kind of talent, a gift, that turned everything he touched into sparkling poetic jewels...

And yet Sal had never published anything.

He had had offers from various presses, but to no avail. He wanted to make it in one of the New Babylonian Press collections and nothing else.

He had never sent them anything.

"I'm just not ready yet," he used to say, with a strange shrug.

And now he was dead.

Unpublished, cold as a stone, rotting.

There was no way to tell whether his death should be considered a victory or a defeat, the poem he had left behind as an explanation was too obscure.

Was it: Poetry 1, Bastards 0, or the other way around?

Not wanting to answer the question, Stefan pressed on.

DEATH

Speck was standing behind his bar, cleaning glasses while the bartenders dealt with the screaming crowd of thirsty customers. In the background you could hear the nerve-wrecking noise of a band called Pussy Violence—Jimmy had seen the poster on the front door—while a stripper tried to keep the beat on an adjacent stage. Lights were mainly red, green and blue. It gave the place atmosphere, Jimmy told himself, lingering on the word. Speck finally noticed the assassin at the other end of the bar and grinned at him. In the light his smile was red too.

POETRY

Children laugh mothers chat
a junkie dies among the flowers
look out children
do not step on the broken shooter
pieces of glass like fake diamonds
—spooky treasure

DOPE

Cassandra was due only later in the evening, so she sat down by the stage at a miraculously empty table and ordered a highball, watching the other girls dance to the screeching sounds of the band.

Sal had disapproved of her working here, but there was no other way: they both needed the money—and besides, she could dance. He had tried to get a job a couple of times himself, but it had been one disaster after another. The only thing he was good at, he claimed, was writing his stuff.

His stuff...

She took a long fizzy sip.

Yeah, his goddamned stuff...

Bright red spotlights drifted from the center of the stage right into her eyes but she didn't blink, just stared back at them.

Sal, the poet.

The Great Unknown Poet.

The dead poet, now.

Big deal.

Tons of them like him everyday.

Literary history was literally overcrowded with dead poets, she remembered from her high school days—but she had never imagined living with one, some day... She had been so bad in literature...

Figure that: Sal's muse was a complete literature imbecile.

She had to admit it was sort of funny, come to think of it...

She drank another sip to cover her painful smile.

The stripper was dancing in the middle of paper flames.

Red fire.

Cassandra thought about this for a second.

Flames.

Yes, she would burn Sal's works tonight.

Make a nice fire of all his words, in the sink.

A funeral pyre.

Words of ashes.

A smoky triumph.

The stripper began to shake her shoulders to make her breasts rotate.

The audience clapped and whistled.

The band ploughed on.

Burn, baby, burn.

DEATH

"Pretty good sound," Jimmy said, pointing at the band over his shoulder.

"Yeah," Speck agreed, with a smile, "and they're getting better all the time. They're signing on a major next week. This is the last time I can afford them. Enjoy... What's bringing you here, anyway? I'm pretty sure it's not the music—you hate music."

They laughed and Jimmy leaned a little forward across the bar counter.

"I want Old Bull's new address."

Speck looked at him with surprise.

"Old Bull? What for?"

Jimmy took a sip from his cold drink and put it back down calmly.

"I need to talk to him."

Speck shook his head.

"That son of a bitch, after all he's written about you..."

Suddenly realizing what it might be all about, a thin smile flashed across the bar owner's face.

"I see, I see... Wait here a second, okay? I'll get it for you. I'll be right back..."

Jimmy made himself more comfortable on his stool as Speck disappeared in a backroom. He liked this place. It had a literary twist to it, although he couldn't quite place it. Maybe he had read something about it, somewhere. A girl sat next to him, pushing his elbow. He turned around and she smiled. She was drunk. Then it hit him: The Gardens of Babylon; the Sonic was described there! Not under its real name, of course—it was called something like the "Boom-Boom Bar"—but nevertheless, it was the place...

A feeling of excitement tickled him as he ordered another drink. So Al Alamein came here... Maybe one day he would be able to meet his favorite writer and convince him to write his true biography... Maybe he had met him here already, without knowing...

The girl collapsed next to him and two bouncers came to pick her up.

"They just can't stand the loud music," Jimmy told the bouncers with a wink.

Speck appeared again waving a piece of paper in his hand.

"There you go: Old Bull's new address... He lives in the suburbs now, near the Moriarty Speedway. It should be pretty easy to find: it's the only house with walled-up windows. Let me know how it went... I'll keep a bottle of champagne aside for the occasion..."

Jimmy thanked him warmly and ordered another drink. They talked for a little while longer, than Speck was called backstage. They warmly shook hands and Jimmy left too.

At the door Nathan was holding a skinny guy by the collar of his shirt.

"You are making me upset," the giant was saying, detaching every word, "and I don't like to be upset..."

Jimmy gave him a friendly tap on the shoulder as he walked past.

"Have a nice day, Nat," he said, climbing on the bike.

Some things really never changed, he told himself, and then he started the bike and was off.

POETRY.

The giant was holding a young man by the neck of his shirt. A bike roared by, almost running Stefan over.

"You are making me very upset," the bouncer repeated.

The man gurgled something then flew in the air, landing with a loud "thud!" on the hood of a car parked in front of the Sonic Bar. He managed to get back up and stumbled away under the blasé looks of the rest in the line.

"Hi Nathan," Stefan said casually when things were over. "How is it going?"

"Business as usual," the bouncer replied, wiping his hands as if they had just been soiled. "What about you? You're working tonight?"

"No, just passing by for a couple of free drinks."

Nathan opened the door for him, flashing a friendly smile.

They had been friends for a while now, since they had been working the door together. Doing a couple nights a week provided Stefan with enough money for rent and food, and besides, he actually kind of liked the job: you could talk about books with Nathan, who was a literature student, and you always met new faces, even if sometimes you had to punch them a little.

DEATH

The sun was shimmering high behind the buildings now.

The address burned in the pocket of Jimmy's leather jacket like a branding iron.

The air slapped his face with its fresh fingers and the rest of the day lay in front of him like a red carpet. Yes, exactly like a soft, red and sticky carpet.

DOPE

"May I join you?"

"Sure..."

Speck took a chair and put another highball on the table.

"This one's on me. Listen, baby, we've got to talk..."

"What about?"

"About you..."

Cassandra put down her glass and leaned back.

"What about me?"

Speck took a deep breath.

"It's not my style to mind other people's business, but for once, honey, I believe I have to make an exception..."

The boss was obviously annoyed.

"In the past, I closed my eyes because you were a good girl and a great dancer, but since Sal's death, man, I don't know, I just don't seem to feel you anymore: you either come in late, or you're so juiced up nobody can talk to you... I can't get a grip, and I don't like that... You know what I mean?"

She picked up the glass again and finished it in a gulp.

Speck was observing her across the table.

His eyes were intense but not mean.

She felt somewhat relieved.

"So in short, I'm asking you to manage your, er, little problem, or I'll be obliged to ask you to quit... This is a clean place, you know..."

She nodded in silence.

Speck got up and gently pinched her cheek as he left the table.

"Good girl…" he said, and disappeared into the crowd.

She was shaking a little.

Good girl, yeah, sure.

She needed this job; that was simple as that.

The blood in her head began to pulse and whirl around.

Her eyes became distant.

This job.

Really?

A golden cloud floated by, illuminating the inside of her forehead. Crystal-pure water ran down her veins, bathing her feet in silver springs.

A job.

No, she didn't need this job after all, or any other.

She bit the glass and broke a piece between her teeth.

Tears appeared at the corner of her eyes but they were not tears of sorrow: they were from laughter.

POETRY

By some extraordinary streak of luck, there was one empty stool at the bar. Stefan pushed his way through and sat down. He ordered a drink from a friend who was bartending.

"Hey, Seanie, do you know if Cassandra's here tonight?"

Seanie nodded.

"She'll be working later. I think she's in here, somewhere... I've seen her, but with all this crowd..."

"Yeah, I can see that. Do you know when her gig is?"

Seanie shrugged negatively. Stefan thanked him and the bartender walked back to the other end of the counter where a beautiful black girl was waiting for him, looking bored.

Stefan turned around to watch the band and the strippers.

Speck had sure understood one thing about life: it was all about sex, booze and rock'n'roll.

The rest was politics.

DEATH

The Moriarty Speedway circled above the building standing alone in the midst of a scrape of barren land, roaring like a mechanical ocean. Old Bull's new hideout had not been very difficult to recognize: as Speck had told him, all the windows of the house had been walled in.

He parked the Indian Chief in front of the steel door, adorned with a bulletproof video camera.

Waving and smiling at the lens, the handsome assassin rang the doorbell.

POETRY

Stefan wondered if he would manage to see Cassandra after her gig. She had been Sal's girlfriend and a junkie like him.

He had mixed feelings towards her. In the one hand, he liked her because she had been the light in Sal's life. On the other hand, she had been too hooked up on dope herself to help him out of it.

Sal had claimed that junk was the fuel of his work. Stefan couldn't accept that. He wanted to believe that Sal had a gift, with or without the stuff. They had often discussed this, but to no avail. Cassandra would never say anything; she was usually too high to realize that anything was going on. She just sat on the bed, her eyes half-closed to the world and a web of spit slowly covering her lower lip.

He put a hand in the inner pocket of his coat and felt the folded paper pages.

He still had Sal's poems on him.

Since his death, he always carried it around.

Eighty-seven pages in all—the only poetry collection he had actually finished. It had no title. He had never sent it.

Stefan sighed and ordered another drink.

Go figure.

Speck was nowhere to be seen. Another stripper appeared on the stage, but it wasn't Cassandra. Maybe he would write her from Saint Petersburg... Maybe he would tell her what he really thought of Sal's talent and how pitiful he thought it was it had had to end that way... Maybe he would try to get Sal's collection published over there... Maybe he was just getting drunk.

He looked at his watch. It was already early evening.

How many drinks?

Enough.

He called Seanie and asked him for a piece of paper and a pen. He wrote a message for Speck:

"Greetings from S. P. Will write you from there. Al."

He would understand.

Cassandra was more difficult.

He finally wrote down what he had wanted to tell her for a long time: "Sal loved you more than junk, baby. Remember him, and remember that. Love, Stefan."

He gave the notes to Seanie and proceeded to struggle back to the entrance door. In a way, he had to admit that he wasn't too disappointed by the fact that he hadn't managed to talk to Speck or Cassandra: goodbyes were really not his thing.

DOPE

The spotlights blinded her as she walked on stage.

All the better, she thought.

A new band began its number.

They were called the Cyberpunk Candles. They were loud and they were good.

The audience of pigs squeezed around her tiny podium, a few feet away from her high-heels. She closed her eyes, letting her body move along the electric riffs and wails. When she opened her eyes again a blinding light soared from beneath her eyelids and illuminated the crowd, which jumped back and gaped in ecstasy.

The heat was on.

The music was slowly growing from a short-circuit into a full forest fire. She could hear the trees crash and scatter in burning shards behind her. Growing, rumbling, roaring, soaring.

The music raged behind her like a red and blue firewall.

The audience was transfixed. Hypnotized.

She could feel the chemistry of chaos starting to boil. Silver bubbles coming up to crackle and pop on the electric surface.

She was noise.

She was a feedback sea goddess.

Dope and music raced through her veins like wild stock cars, zooming in her head again and again and again.

Somebody in the audience began to freak and dropped to the ground, screaming and foaming at the mouth.

She heard someone say "epilepsy."

It could have been the name of the song.

She spread her thighs wide open right under the nose of a pale pimply kid glittering with sweat.

Hands reached out to touch her.

She saw the bouncers come running into the thickening crowd. The first blows were exchanged. One of the guitarists cranked the amps. A chair flew in the distance. Someone grabbed her ankle and she kicked him back in the face.

Waves of white noise and feedback caressed her back.

She thrust her hips forwards, taking off her golden panties in a slow gyrating motion, although she knew it was forbidden to show pubes in here.

An empty bottle circled in the air and crashed against the wall behind the bass player.

A blanket of sweat wrapped her shoulders.

Her sex filled up with sticky electricity.

She began to caress herself with a bottle that had rolled on her podium.

There were screams in the audience, there were more blows.

A microphone fell down. Feedback arrows pierced skulls and heads. Rage wasn't a word, rage was a sound.

Broken bones; shattered teeth; crushed balls.

Yes yes yes yes yes.

She began to laugh.

She had finally found the exit.

First door after the flames.

DEATH

"Jimmy! What a surprise!"

The old man greeted him with open arms and hugged him briefly. "The Kiss Of Death," Jimmy remembered with anguish. Old Bull was famous for this. He would pretend to recognize his victim, open his arms or extend a hand and shoot them. It was very efficient¾Speedy Jimmy had himself successfully experimented the trick a couple of times.

He took a few steps back, happy to be still alive, and looked at the old assassin standing in front of him. Old Bull was wearing a silk bathrobe decorated with two grinning dragons barely concealing a heavy gun hanging in a shoulder strap. His eyes were circled with his ageless steel-rimmed glasses and his smile was the same old reptile smile he remembered so well.

A young blond man walked in, whom Old Bull introduced as his current "secretary," with a heavy wink. They all sat down on an Arab couch, in front of a huge TV set almost crumbling under a mountain of videotapes.

"Personal stuff," Bulldog explained, answering Jimmy's unspoken question. "What brings you here, anyway? Oh, let me guess... the book! Yes, it must be the book..."

Jimmy felt his jaws lock with rage and his fists close tightly. No, not yet, he told himself, not yet...

POETRY

Once in the streets again, Stefan took a deep breath and resumed his walk. He felt the letter and the plane ticket in his pocket. What choice did he have? It was quite simple, actually: stay here and eventually spend the rest of his life in prison, or go away and live in peace. The answer sounded obvious—but it wasn't.

No, not at all.

It was true, yes, that it was extremely dangerous to be published illegally in Babylon, but he had always written about this city.

It was his own gigantic muse.

It was the ink in his pen, the blood in his veins, the booze in his glass, the sperm in his balls...

Could he possibly live without it?

The pen was easy enough to bring along but could he ever find the same ink?

He walked inside a grocery store and bought himself another quart of liquor. This, at least, you could find everywhere, except in Teheran, but then again, who fucking cared?

DOPE

Nathan helped her with her coat outside.

"We're all going to miss you here," he said, giving her a quick hug.

It was like embracing a sequoia tree, she thought.

He spat on the ground and looked away.

"Well, it's time to say goodbye, now," she said after a moment of silence.

"I guess so," the giant replied, still not looking at her.

She could see he was moved and that turned her stomach too. She gave him a quick kiss on the cheek. Nathan smiled awkwardly like a shy grizzly bear and walked back inside. She heard the sound of the lock and saw his big paw hang the "Sorry, we're closed" sign behind the glass-pane.

One door closed, a few more to go.

DEATH

"Here, have this. It'll make you feel better..."

Jimmy took the joint from Old Bull's hand and inhaled deeply. Something like a refreshing autumn breeze immediately filled his lungs.

"What is this stuff?" he asked, amazed at the swift effect of the drug.

"Personal blend," Bulldog answered with a mysterious smile. "A secret, if you will."

The young blond man took a drag in his turn and passed it back to the old man. The veteran assassin inhaled and began to laugh quietly, all his face frozen in a demented grin.

Jimmy recognized this face as soon as he saw it.

He had encountered it many times before in his life.

It was the happy mask of Death.

DOPE

At the corner of the street, Cassandra counted the bills.

Speck had given all he had owed her, which was nice of him considering the number of glasses, chairs and tables he would have to replace—notwithstanding the entire sound system, which short-circuited after a full bottle of vodka had crashed on a live wire... Oh well, what a finale, though.

The streets were dark now.

A full moon had risen over the skyline.

She counted her money again and hailed a passing cab.

In this peculiar light, it looked like a beautiful hearse.

DEATH

"I don't like your book," Jimmy finally said. "I don't like it at all..."

"Why?"

"It's full of lies."

"Such as...?"

"I never slept with you to get that job."

The old man lit another joint and blew the smoke through his nose.

"Oh yes, you did."

"What the hell are you talking about?"

"You, come here," Old Bull intimated to his "secretary," who moved up one seat and was now hip to hip with his boss. Old Bull put down his joint, took the young blond man in his arms and kissed him passionately, rubbing an open hand against his crotch.

"You want? You want now?"

The young man shook his head with adoration.

"Well, you'll have to wait, amor, we have company..."

Old Bull kissed the boy one more time on the lips, then picked up the joint resting on the ashtray.

"Just like that. You slept with me just like that and that's why I took you into the Guild. I know that. You know that. Now everybody knows that..."

"According to your goddamned book!"

"I made you famous, my beautiful Jimmy, I made you famous..."

"You didn't make me anything!"

Old Bull began to unbutton the blond man's shirt and ran a smooth hand on the offered chest.

"Oh yes, I did. You wouldn't be anybody if you hadn't slept with me. I taught you everything: how to shoot, how to write and how to read. I am your Pygmalion; face it once and for all. And now, you are the hero of my book. MY hero. You are nothing by yourself. Nothing at all."

"NOOOOOOOOOOOOOOOO!"

Jimmy's scream echoed in the room and the young blond man began to giggle as Old Bull licked his ear. Jimmy tried to get up but the room began to spin like a crazy wheel and he fell backwards onto the dark-blue rollercoaster couch of unconsciousness.

POETRY

The streets were still warm although it was evening.

Stefan stopped in front of a gun shop and looked at the weapons displayed. There was a beautiful.45 glistening in the orange neon light. A bullet in the head might have helped solve his problems...

He shivered. Did he really want to end up like Sal? Cold and unknown forever? His dedication to the written word wasn't that absolute.

He took a sip of whisky from the bottle and walked on, shaking his head.

The plane ticket in his pocket had suddenly made him entirely bulletproof.

DOPE

"Take all this money and drive for as long as it lasts," she told the driver through the tinted bulletproof glass.

"Any particular direction?"

"No, just drive around town. Anywhere..."

"Sure, but this is a hell of a lot of money you know? I could drive until dawn with this..."

"Then do it," she concluded, shutting the security window with a dry snap. She felt the car shiver and swerve towards dawn. The shooter was ready in her purse, filled to the rim with its bag-and-a-half worth of junk. A rocket trip to dawn. Speed on, driver, speed on ... one can never arrive too early to the beginning of a brand new day.

POETRY

Louise was standing at her usual corner. It seemed as if she had been waiting for him. Stefan knew he was very drunk. He hoped she wouldn't mind but, then again, she was probably used to this by now. Better be.

"Hello, Louise."

His voice sounded thick and uneasy.

"Hi, Stefan. Wanna go up for a little while?"

He nodded. His neck hurt. His whole body hurt. She grabbed him by he arm and they walked off together. He could feel that she was almost carrying him, an all too familiar scene which made him feel ashamed.

They climbed the steep stairs to her little apartment.

He was toiling at every step but she patiently helped him. When they finally got to her bedroom, she let him crash on the bed.

"Louise, I've got... I've got to talk to you..."

She lay next to him and said she was listening.

He didn't know where to begin. She had been his secret muse for all this time and he had to abandon her now. The idea was making him sick inside but he had to tell her. She deserved to know the truth—that he loved her and that he had to leave. He had an obligation to speak to her. And he did.

She listened to him, all night.

Once in a while she would get up and check if her kid was all right in the other room.

When the first lights of dawn peeked through the window, she finally said, "I understand," and he saw there was no need for another word.

DEATH

The door to the room opened and a beautiful naked girl stepped in. Jimmy couldn't really distinguish her features, but she was tall and slim. They were alone. The two others had mysteriously disappeared.

She kneeled at his feet and untied his belt.

Jimmy let her, enjoying the softness of her hands.

She dragged his pants down and proceeded with his underpants.

Jimmy let out a quiet growl.

Lifting his T-shirt, she began to lick him all the way down to his groin.

When she finally wrapped his throbbing member with her soft lips, Jimmy told himself with a mixture of satisfaction and wonder that with Old Bull, you really never knew what was going to come next.

POETRY

Louise was sitting at her dressing table, fixing her earrings while he gathered his clothes. She had called him a taxi. It would be here in a few minutes. A new day had begun.

She was letting him go because she loved him.

The blessing of the Muse.

He thought of a poem, but it flickered away.

He promised her that he would send her money as soon as possible, so that she could join him in Saint Petersburg. She said that he would probably find another Louise there. He didn't answer. The taxi honked twice outside. There was no coming back, now.

Take the pen and forget about the ink.

He kissed her one last time. He felt her tears stick to his cheek.

"Take good care of yourself," she whispered.

He promised he would write her but she put her fingers to his lips. When the door shut behind him, he knew he would never forget Louise: she would always have for him the sad and tragic eyes of Babylon.

DOPE

The driver stopped the car at the corner of the street where he had picked up the girl. He figured she wouldn't mind being back where she had started.

"Hey, miss, we're here!" he said once through the security window. He waited for an answer but nothing came. Looking in his rearview mirror, all he could see through the tinted glass was her slouched body.

"She must have fallen asleep," he told himself, and he stepped out to open her door.

A very white arm fell through the opening of the door and something dropped on the hard ground, where it broke with a crystal-clear sound.

"Shit," the man muttered between his teeth, "shit, shit, shit, shit!"

There was no pulse in the wrist he was holding.

A car whooshed by. Then another. And another.

The flow went on, getting thicker minute by minute, like a blind river running endlessly towards another day of work and eternity.

The driver called the cops from a pay-phone at the corner of the street and while he waited for them, he decided that it was about time he quit this goddamned job altogether.

DEATH

When Jimmy woke up, his pants were down and he was coming in Old Bull's warm mouth.

"Holy shit!" he exclaimed, paralyzed with disgust and surprise.

As he struggled to free himself from the old man's grip, he heard a sound which made him turn his head.

The young blond man was filming the scene with a portable video camera.

Jimmy felt his stomach bang against his back teeth. He finally managed to push back the lust-ridden Bulldog and, grabbing his gun, shot at the camera, which exploded in a mixture of blood, glass and plastic.

Old Bull's desperate scream filled the room.

Jimmy saw the heavy.44 jump in the old man's hand, but too late. It barked twice, throwing the young assassin back against the couch, as if he had been punched by two giant fists. In spite of the shock, he managed to shoot again and Old Bull flew with his back against the wall, his chest spraying red paint all around him.

The old assassin slowly slid to the ground, leaving a dark and sticky trail on the white plaster behind him.

Jimmy felt a metallic taste in his mouth and he began to throw up a mixture of blood and saliva.

He tried to feel his gut but his hands wouldn't move.

He was feeling very cold and he began shivering.

"Shit!" he whispered, "shit!"

There was nothing he could do about anything anymore.

He had been Old Bull's character until the end, or so it seemed, and nobody would ever know the truth now. They would only believe what they would see—and what his dying eyes were staring at in horror—which were Old Bull's priapic erection emerging from the robe, pointing at his direction like an accusing finger and the peaceful snake-smiling mouth, still glistening with the sperm of the late and famous Speedy Jimmy.

POETRY

Below the wing of the plane lay Babylon, flat and grey like a piece of antique sidewalk. Stefan looked at it for a moment, until he felt a presence by his side. A beautiful blonde stewardess asked him with a charming smile if he cared for anything to drink.

He ordered a double scotch on the rocks and looked down again, but Babylon had vanished in the meantime, eaten forever by the thick white clouds which rolled under the plane like the big chunks of ice sometimes carried by the River Styx in spring.

SPECIAL THANKS

Pussy Violence and Cyberpunk Candles appear courtesy of Native Violence Records, copyright NVR, 1997.

The poems are excerpts from Forgetting Babylon, by Stefan Marcovitch, copyright Yellow Rose Press, Saint Petersburg, 1998.